Promise Me Please, Cowboy

Promise Me Please, Cowboy

The 85th Copper Mountain Rodeo series

C.J. Carmichael

Promise Me Please, Cowboy
Copyright© 2023 C.J. Carmichael
Tule Publishing First Printing, September 2023

The Tule Publishing, Inc.

ALL RIGHTS RESERVED

First Publication by Tule Publishing 2023

Cover design by Lee Hyat Designs

No part of this book may be used or reproduced in any manner whatsoever without written permission except in the case of brief quotations embodied in critical articles and reviews.

This is a work of fiction. Names, characters, places, and incidents are products of the author's imagination or are used fictitiously. Any resemblance to actual events, locales, organizations, or persons, living or dead, is entirely coincidental.

ISBN: 978-1-961544-10-9

Dedication

For Megan, word spinner extraordinaire, who takes the pictures and supplies the sound tracks.

For Lillian, who was there at the beginning,

For Sinclair, who adds all the sparkles,

For Meghan who, with grace and skill, turns manuscripts into books in readers' hands,

Most of all for Jane, the instigator who never gives up, who believes in stories and women and champions both.

Chapter One

CHET HARDWICK GAZED dubiously at the exterior of the Bramble House B & B. The yard was unkempt, with an overgrown lawn, shaggy shrubbery and flower beds taken over by weeds. The house itself, a three-story brick Victorian, was in good shape though. It looked like the sort of place that would have bouquets of wildflowers in every room, tea and cookies in the parlor, and expensive chocolates on the plumped-up pillows at night. It was probably run by an older couple who would ask too many questions, or worse, talk incessantly about their grandchildren. The breakfast would be a sit-down affair forcing him to mingle with a bunch of strangers before his first cup of coffee, and to eat with his elbows off the table.

Stay at the Bramble House B & B? He'd rather sleep in the barn with his horses, thank you very much.

Unfortunately, his old rodeo friends Sage Carrigan and her husband Dawson O'Dell who had suggested Chet compete in the rodeo in Marietta, Montana, this year *and* had offered to put him up in their spare bedroom, had received an unexpected visit from Dawson's mother and her current husband. End result was that while Chet's horses were still welcome at Sage's sister's Circle C ranch there was no room for Chet. Instead, Sage had made reservations for him here. At the Bramble House B & B. Which supposedly was one of the top-rated places in town.

Which was probably why it was hate at first sight for him.

Chet did not stay at top-rated places. Mostly he camped or if the weather was especially miserable he might splurge on a budget motel. For Chet, comfort was a state of mind, not a pricey mattress with a fluffy duvet that was too white for him to put his feet on.

But Sage had prepaid here through to Sunday, so he'd need to get her money back before he moved someplace more to his liking. Reluctantly he set out on the path that cut through the overgrown lawn to the front porch. In his opinion a good porch needed a rocking chair and a table where you could rest your coffee mug when you weren't drinking from it. The chair did not need a cushion—simple was best.

But this porch was not simple. It had more furniture than most living rooms he'd seen—and all the chairs were cushioned. There were baskets and tubs full of flowers and even a small water fountain in one corner. It would have made a perfect magazine cover except that the flowers had wilted in the hot afternoon air.

The front door was ajar—perhaps because of the beautiful weather—and as he opened it wide before stepping inside, a musical chime sounded. From the hallway beyond the foyer he heard a woman swear.

"Damn! Ouch! Damn!"

He almost grinned. That was a welcome that made him feel right at home. "Hello to you too."

"Sorry about that. You caught me…at a bad moment." A twenty-something woman was on the top rung of a stepladder, with a light bulb in hand. A broken light bulb, he saw, as he stepped closer. Blood dripped from one of her fingers.

"I can come back another time." But even as he said this, he was moving toward the ladder and reaching out to steady it.

"No, no, that's fine. Hang on." She descended awkwardly, using just one hand, the other still holding the ill-fated bulb. "The old one burnt out, but now I've broken the new one and it was the last in the package."

She made this sound like a tragedy of the highest order.

Dramatic, he decided. Also, cute, with long, messy, curly blonde hair and round intense blue eyes, which looked worried at the moment.

He grabbed the wastebasket from behind the desk—which was tucked into an alcove created by the grand staircase—and gestured for her to drop the broken bulb inside. Then he handed her a clean handkerchief. "You're bleeding. Use this."

She blanched at the sight of her own blood and quickly

covered the cut with the square of cotton.

"I thought handkerchiefs were extinct. As well as the type of man who would carry one."

"You can thank my grandmother. She had a thing against tissues." His grandmother, the one person he had loved with all his heart, the one person who had felt the same about him, had died when he was eight, but not before instilling in him her strong views on many topics, not just handkerchiefs. Views about good manners and honesty and looking before you leapt. The last came in particularly handy when you made your living as a rodeo cowboy.

On the afternoon of his grandmother's funeral, while the adults were eating and drinking and being boring in her living room, Chet had found a stash of her handkerchiefs in her night side table. He'd stuffed them into his pockets. Hidden them from his father. Carried them with him as they traveled from town to town, rodeo to rodeo, motel room to motel room. The cotton squares smelled like his grandmother and he buried his face in them at night to help him fall asleep.

Lilies. They had smelled like lilies.

"Step outside where the light is better so I can get a look at your hand."

She stood rooted in place, looking at him like he'd suggested the two of them go rob a bank.

"There could be bits of glass in your finger."

"That's fine. I can take care of it later." She gave him a

closer look. "You must be the rodeo cowboy Sage Carrigan reserved a room for. Chet Hardwick."

"What gave me away?" He glanced down at his western shirt, jeans and favorite boots.

"Not exactly a mental leap, was it? I'm Amy Arden, the new owner of Bramble House. Let me sign you in and show you to your room."

As she moved toward the desk, he noticed she had a slight limp. He also caught a whiff of her perfume. Something sweet and exotic. He wanted to move closer, instead he took a step back.

"Owner? Aren't you a little young?" In his mind he was paying her a compliment, but she seemed affronted.

"I've got an undergrad degree in finance from Cornell and a master's from Harvard. I suppose I'm qualified to run a small-town bed-and-breakfast."

It took a few moments to absorb her impressive credentials. "Overqualified, some would say."

She glanced back at her finger. "And yet it seems I can't change a simple light bulb."

"You might need a PhD for that. Or…you could just ask a cowboy."

"But that was the last bulb," she reminded him. "I'll have to order more on Amazon."

"You could just head over to the local hardware store. Take fifteen minutes tops."

"Right."

City girl, he figured. "New York?" he guessed.

"Born and raised."

"So…what brings you to Montana?"

"Good question," he was sure he heard her mutter, before she said with what he felt sure was fake cheerfulness, "Fresh air and wide-open spaces."

"Right." There had to be more to her story. Not that it mattered to him. "Look, I'm sure you're busy so—"

"Busy, that's an understatement. I'm supposed to be in the kitchen baking cookies by now. And making a fresh pot of coffee. But I had three rooms to clean and prepare for guests this morning and it put me behind."

The place was so quiet. She seemed to be the only one here. "Don't you have staff?"

"There was staff when I bought the place. But…" Out came her fake-cheerful voice again: "I'm doing it all now. Gardens, laundry, cleaning and *baking*." She emphasized the latter item, as if it was the baking that really had pushed her over the edge. "As well as bookings, paperwork, and regular maintenance."

"That's a lot."

"Damn right." She bit her lip. "Sorry. I shouldn't be swearing in front of a guest. Or complaining. It's just, I'm used to being competent at my job. More than competent, actually." She sighed. "Do you mind signing the guest register?" She held up her injured right hand. "I don't want to get any blood on it. Sage asked me to reserve the Blue room for you. It has the best view of Copper Mountain."

With her left hand she'd grabbed a key from one of the desk drawers. She glanced down at the register book, which he still hadn't signed. "Is there a problem?"

"I came in here to cancel the reservation. Sage meant well and all, but I'm not a bed-and-breakfast kind of guy."

"Not a bed-and-breakfast kind of guy," she said softly. "What is that supposed to mean?"

He took another backward step. "No offence. I just—"

"I may be new at the job, but the beds are clean and comfortable and the breakfast is hearty enough for the largest appetite."

"I usually just have coffee in the morning. And I'm sure your beds are great, but my tastes are simple. I'd be happier in a barn than a bed-and-breakfast."

"A barn." She looked at him as if he was nuts. "Not a fan of indoor plumbing?"

"A lot of barns have that."

"For the animals?"

"For the people who look after them. Look, if you'd just refund Sage's money... I assume she paid by credit card?"

Amy crossed her arms over her chest, his grandmother's handkerchief still wound around her index finger. "I'm sorry, but if you check our website, you'll see there are no refunds within forty-eight hours of your stay. This past week I turned down several reservation requests for your room. Sage told me you'd be staying through to the end of rodeo weekend.

Have your plans changed?"

He was floored by the forty-eight-hour policy. Was that a thing? He wasn't the kind of guy who booked hotel rooms—or restaurants for that matter. He took what was available or he moved on.

He became aware that Amy Arden was now anxiously working a silver bracelet up and down her arm like a horse fighting a bit. Sounded like she was having some adjustment issues with her new business, and he didn't want to add to her problems. But he hated feeling cornered into doing something that made him uncomfortable.

"Yeah, I'm here for the rodeo. Which is exactly my point. When I'm competing I need to focus. I can't be making chitchat with strangers around the breakfast table. I need to be taking care of my horses, not munching cookies and tea in some fancy parlor."

Amy stared at him for several moments. Then she went to the drawer and exchanged one key for another. "How about this. I've got a room over the garage. It's in the process of being repainted—the guys I hired suddenly got a bigger project and left with the job half-done—but if you don't mind a little mess, you can stay there. It's got a separate entrance so you won't run into any of the other guests. I'll bring you up a thermos of coffee and some muffins in the morning and leave them outside your door. You won't even have to deal with me."

He'd still rather be someplace cheap and simple. But it

was nice of her to try and accommodate him. "Add a little straw and a water trough and you've got a deal."

She stared at him.

"That was a joke."

"It better be. We have a strict no straw policy at Bramble House."

AMY HAD NEVER met anyone like Chet Hardwick. Since moving to Marietta she'd grown accustomed to seeing men and women dressed western from their hats to their boots. But none had worn the garb like it was their second skin, and none of the men had made her feel like she was looking at a young Clint Eastwood—only not an actor, the real deal.

Everything about Chet felt real. Authentic. The man did not bend to accommodate others. Being around him made her miss her old self, the one who had blazed through life fearlessly, whether she was running a marathon or closing a business deal or out on a date with a handsome guy.

It had been more than a year now since she'd felt that confidence and she missed it.

"Come with me and I'll show you the room."

She didn't look, but she could hear his cowboy boots on the wood floor, so she knew he was following her as she went outside. She paused for a moment on the porch. The flowers needed watering. The lawn mowing.

At least the view was still stunning. It had been three weeks and she still couldn't get over the piercing blue of the sky. On the other side of the street, the pristine Marietta River flowed and beyond that were the majestic Absaroka mountains.

"Quite the setting," Chet said.

"It is. A big change from the brick wall our New York apartment looked out on." In the evening when she stole a moment to sit out here and enjoy the setting sun, Amy could almost convince herself that moving here hadn't been a mistake.

Almost.

She took the stairs carefully. She was still getting used to the way her legs worked post-surgery and didn't want to risk a fall. On the path to the garage, Chet asked her to wait a minute.

"Let me see your finger."

She hesitated. She could tell by the throbbing pain that there was still some glass in there. But Chet was a guest and she could deal with it on her own. "It's fine."

"I may not look like it, but I've got a delicate touch. Fished many a thorn from a good dog's paw. Not one of them complained."

"You have a dog?" He hadn't mentioned a pet at check-in, but it wouldn't be a problem.

"Been around dogs all my life, but never had one of my own." Before she could protest again, he unwrapped the cloth from her finger. "Yup. There's a piece of glass in here all right."

Her mother's silver bracelet slid down her arm as he raised her finger toward the sunlight. Amy didn't have the stomach to look at her bleeding finger. So she focused on Chet's eyes instead. Unlike Clint Eastwood, Chet's eyes were brown, like melting milk chocolate. For a hard man, he sure had soft eyes. And an even softer touch. She didn't feel a thing as he removed the shard of glass, except relief from the pain.

"Thank you." As she brought her wounded hand in close to her heart, the sunlight caught the silver of her bracelet, sending a shaft of light to her eyes and reminding her to step back. "The room," she said, more to orient herself than anything else.

He followed her up the stairs and she unlocked the door, hoping the painters hadn't left a big mess. She hadn't been up here since they'd informed her they couldn't finish the job—about the same time Jo, Ella and Robert had walked out on her.

Their dramatic resignations had come at the end of her first orientation meeting. All she'd done was suggest a few minor décor and menu changes, and they'd bolted like rats off a sinking ship. Except Bramble House wasn't sinking.

At least not yet.

She pushed open the door and was instantly relieved. The painters had left their supplies on a tarp in one corner of the space and the baseboards were outlined with green tape, but other than that, the room was tidy. Yes, half of the walls were a calming taupe while the others were still fern green, but surely Chet wouldn't care about that.

"This is fine," he said. "I'll settle in later. First I need to drive out to the Circle C and take care of my horses."

"How many do you travel with?"

"Just two. Bourbon and Hunter. Beautiful quarter horses, both of them."

She couldn't imagine a life where you traveled with two horses. "Where do you live? When you're not on the road?"

"I'm almost always on the road. But in the winter I work at a ranch in Boulder."

"Is that where your family is, then?"

"No family." His mouth hardened. "At least none worth speaking about."

Me either, she thought sadly. Like her bum leg, that was another thing she was having a difficult time getting used to.

Chapter Two

CHET ENJOYED THE thirty-minute drive back to the Circle C. The ranch was nestled into the aptly named Paradise Valley, through which flowed the Yellowstone River as it traveled the divide between the Absarokas and the Gallatins. This was prime cattle ranching territory with grazing lands stretching back from the valley up to the flanks of the mountains themselves. He was grateful Sage's sister Callan and Callan's husband Court had been willing to put up his horses for the duration. He only wished they'd offered him a bed in their bunkhouse too. He didn't understand why Sage had thought he needed accommodations as nice as the B & B. But given that it had all been paid for—and couldn't be refunded—he supposed he would have to try and enjoy it.

His thoughts circled back to the new owner. The very pretty and surprisingly young new owner. She was a puzzle. Why would someone with her education leave all her family and friends in New York to buy a bed-and-breakfast in small-town Marietta? And why had her staff all quit…because he was certain she hadn't chosen to do all that work on her own? She was clearly over her head, stressed and anxious. The type of person he normally avoided.

Yet there had been moments of connection. And attraction. He liked her sense of humor. How nice she'd smelled up close. The hidden strength in her delicate hand.

Amy wore lots of silver rings, but none on her wedding finger. She'd made it sound like she had lived with someone in New York. Could have been a roommate, or a boyfriend. Perhaps it was a love affair gone wrong that had sent her running off to Montana.

He knew from songs and movies how painful a breakup could be, though he had never experienced it himself. His affairs were casual and brief. Partly because of his vagabond life—so like his father's even though he'd hated it growing up—and partly out of preference. He treated women kindly and with respect, but he also held them at a distance. Or so he'd been told.

He was surprised to see he'd reached the gate with the Circle C brand. He was already here and instead of enjoying the scenery he'd spent most of his time thinking about Amy Arden. That struck him as foolish.

A woman like Amy would have no interest in a simple cowboy like him, and he had no business investing any of his feelings in a woman like her.

Chet had dropped his horses off only hours ago, yet in the intervening time several new vehicles had been parked out front of the sprawling two-story log house. Three of the trucks were local, while another had Flathead County plates and a fourth, a large SUV, came from Washington State. Callan had told him her sisters and their families usually came home for the rodeo. Looked like a bunch of them had showed up early.

Chet drove past the house and parked near the barns. Bourbon and Hunter were in the pen where he'd left them, standing in the shade of some old cottonwoods, grazing laconically. They perked up when they heard him whistle, came trotting to welcome him.

He nuzzled them both before leading the way to the stable. He'd give them each some light exercise, a good brushing and a feeding, before making his way back to town for his own supper. The enticing aroma of a hickory smoker wafted from the back of the Carrigans' ranch house.

He glanced over and saw what looked like at least a dozen adults and a crew of teenagers, children and babies, gathered on the patio and spilling out to the expansive lawns beyond. They were several hundred yards away. He doubted any of them even noticed him as he paused to wonder what it must be like, to have such a big family.

Laughter burst out frequently, along with shouts from the children, and the occasional baby's cry. By all accounts they seemed to be having a really good time.

Montana summer days were long and Chet took his time with his horses. Fact was, despite his rising hunger, he'd rather be here with them than eating supper alone. He was cleaning tack when he heard someone enter the barn. He smiled when he saw it was Sage. Her long red hair was in a thick braid and looking at her youthful face, you'd never guess she was near forty.

"Hey, Chet."

He'd been a teenager when he'd first met Sage. She'd been a high-ranking barrel racer back then, and he'd been a novice tie-down roper, beneath her notice, but she'd been kind to him. She'd noticed the way he hung back, took his meals alone, generally kept to himself.

And she'd gone out of her way to befriend him. When most people found out who his father was—Walt Hardwick had a reputation on the rodeo circuit as a shady character and an angry drunk—most people were apprehensive. Not Sage. When he admitted he was Walt Hardwick's son she'd been kinder still.

"You take real good care of your horses," she said now.

"They deserve it."

"I'm sure they do, but what about you? We've got smoked brisket and baked beans and my grandmother's famous coleslaw back at the house. How about you come and join us?"

Chet had met all kinds of folks in the rodeo world. Some were wild, more interested in booze and drugs and women, than their careers. After seeing what too much drink had done for his old man, Chet generally steered away from this crowd.

Others, the majority, were friendly people with good morals and respectful manners. From this group Chet had often been extended invitations to join various families for dinners or holidays. In his late teens and early twenties he used to accept these invitations until he noticed how depressed he felt after. Because as friendly as those folks always were, they were not his family, and at the end of the day he was still alone.

Truth was, it hurt too much to see what other people had and what he did not.

"I'm fine. Probably grab a burger in town before I turn in. Thanks for booking me a room at the bed-and-breakfast, by the way. It's a real nice place."

"It was while my family owned it. I hope it stays that way."

He could hear doubt in her voice. "You don't think Amy Arden is up to the job?"

"I'm not sure. No one in the family met her before she came out here to take possession. We hadn't realized she was so young. Or that she'd never even been to Montana before."

"She told me she was from New York City."

"Yes. Used to work on Wall Street, apparently."

"It's quite a leap from there to here," he agreed. And like his grandmother always said, you should look before you leap. He wondered if Amy had done that. Based on what he'd seen today, she hadn't.

"It certainly is. And she didn't help her situation when

she sat her staff down on the first day and told them all the changes she wanted to make."

"I take it they all quit?"

Sage raised her eyebrows. "That's right. Jo and Ella had been working at Bramble House for years, ever since my great-aunt Mable opened it up for business. Naturally they feel vested in the history of the place. They took Amy's ideas as criticism of the way they'd been doing things."

Chet moved the saddle he'd been buffing to a storage rack. He wiped his hands on a rag then glanced back at Sage. "What changes does Amy have in mind?"

"I'm not sure, to be honest. I do know she wanted to remove the family photos and replace them with generic western art."

That didn't sound too audacious to Chet. But he kept his mouth closed.

Sage followed him to his truck. "I really wish you'd stay for dinner. I feel so badly about offering you our guest room and then bailing at the last minute."

"That's okay. Family first. I get that."

She looked uncomfortable. "Dawson's mother is a bit of a prima donna. If we'd told her we didn't have room for her, she'd have thrown a fit. Frankly I might have done it anyway, but Dawson puts up with the Carrigan clan all the time. So on the rare occasions his mother visits I try to be as accommodating as possible."

He patted her shoulder. "It's all good, Sage. I am going

to insist, though, that you let me pay you back for the bed-and-breakfast."

"No way, Chet." She backed away. "Dawson and I agreed, it's the least we can do. We're looking forward to cheering you on at the rodeo by the way. And you have to join us for the Saturday night barbecue."

"Aw, I usually skip those things."

"Not this time. And you better come to the Sunday breakfast, too. Dawson and I will be flipping pancakes."

"I'll be there," he promised. And he would. He'd fill his plate, eat his chow, and then leave. And no one would miss him when he was gone.

AMY DIDN'T KNOW why she found the cowboy from this afternoon so fascinating. She was not one of those girls who had been horse (or boy) crazy when she was young. She thought rodeos were guilty of animal cruelty, and she rarely ate red meat. Most of her meals were vegetarian. When you got down to it, the values of a cowboy were exactly opposite to hers, so why did she keep picturing Chet Hardwick's gentle brown eyes? Why could she still feel his touch on her arm from when he'd tended to her bloody finger?

After he'd left she'd put his cotton handkerchief to soak in cold water, and then baked a batch of chocolate chip cookies. She'd followed the recipe closely. *Exactly.*

And they had turned out the way they had the other four times she'd tried. Spread out into thin blobs over the cookie sheet, like paper dolls holding hands (and touching heads and feet as well). They bore no resemblance to cookies. So straight into the garbage they went. And straight downtown went she.

Fortunately there was an excellent bakery in town where she could load up on gourmet cookies, but while they were delicious and looked beautiful, they were also pricey. She could imagine the bite she was taking out of her profit margin as she handed over her credit card.

Next stop was the Copper Mountain Chocolate Shop. According to the operating binder Eliza had left for her, it was customary to place cowboy-boot-shaped chocolates on the pillows as part of the turndown service. This, Amy thought, was an unnecessary extravagance, but until she had time to drive to the Costco in Bozeman and purchase some large-volume chocolates with a much lower per unit cost, she had no choice but to shop here.

So she entered the shop, determined to resist the rich aromas of chocolate and vanilla and caramel and only buy what was needed for her business.

But she was surrounded by temptation. Salted caramel chocolates here. Chocolate mint meltaways there. No matter where she looked, she saw something else to lust after. The chocolates didn't just smell delicious, they looked gorgeous, too, each one an individual piece of art.

To one side of the store was a seating area, where customers could enjoy their tasty treats at leisure. There were only a few empty seats that she could see. Despite their high prices, Copper Mountain Chocolates obviously did a good business.

"May I help you?" A pretty woman with a heart-shaped face and curvy figure came out of the back room. She was wearing a copper-colored apron and a friendly smile.

"Hi, yes. I'm Amy Arden the new owner of the Bramble House B & B."

The woman's eyebrows arched, and it seemed to Amy that her smile cooled a few degrees. Still, her response was pleasant.

"Nice to meet you. I'm Portia Bradshaw. My grandmother on my mother's side grew up in Bramble House."

"Oh. So you're related to Eliza then? And her great-aunt Mable?"

"Yes. There are a lot of us Carrigan-Brambles around town. I have to admit we were sad to see the old house sold out of the family. But none of us had the time or money to invest in running the B & B. That's life right? Things change."

Boy do they ever, thought Amy. But all she did was nod.

"Speaking of change," Portia continued, her voice more tentative now, "I hear you plan to shake things up a bit at the B & B."

Amy supposed she shouldn't be surprised that the old

staff had been gossiping about her around town. Jeez, all she'd done was suggest some new artwork, a little paint, and some vegetarian breakfast items. Had that really been worth quitting over? Maybe the staff simply hadn't liked her. Whatever the reason, it had been a blow having them all quit. And it felt even worse knowing she was the outsider and everyone in town was already judging her.

"To be honest, I'm too busy to change much yet. Which is why I'm here for the usual order of chocolate cowboy boots. According to the operating binder Eliza left me, we have a standing order every month?"

It would have been nice if Eliza and her husband Marshall had been on hand to answer some of Amy's questions in person. But they had already taken jobs managing a remote mountain lodge in Colorado. At least Eliza had put together the binder for her. It had become Amy's bible. In it Eliza had itemized the daily, weekly and seasonal tasks of running the B & B. She'd also provided names and contact information for suppliers as well as dozens of her guests' favorite recipes.

"Yes. We weren't sure if you were going to carry on with that tradition, but Sage asked me to prepare the order for you just in case." Portia went to the back room and returned with a copper-colored bag containing several large boxes.

As Amy reached for the bag, Portia noticed her bracelet.

"Oh, that's pretty. Montana sapphires are so beautiful, aren't they? Did you buy the bracelet here?"

"It was my mother's." Amy took a closer look. A row of mountains were engraved in the silver band, and over them, sparkling like stars, were six cornflower-blue stones. "Are these Montana sapphires?"

"I'm not an expert, but I think so. They look just like the stones in my aunt Callan's ring." Portia paused to think. "Montana sapphires are pretty rare. Do you know where your mother got her bracelet from? Was she ever in Montana?"

Amy did know. It was all information she'd learned this past year, in the aftermath of losing her mother. But she wasn't about to share. She'd provided enough entertainment for the town grapevine. She didn't want to give them more to talk about.

Chapter Three

THE SUN WAS low on the horizon when Chet stepped into Grey's Saloon to grab a burger. The place was moderately busy for a Tuesday night. A trio at the bar—a young woman and two men—seemed to be attracting a lot of attention from the local cowboys. Chet headed away from them choosing a booth in the back corner. All he wanted was a burger and a cup of coffee and then a good night's sleep.

A server came quickly to take his order. "Place is hopping tonight," he said. "There's a documentary film crew here from Seattle. They're doing a story on the history of rodeo."

No wonder the cowboys were flocking. No doubt looking for a moment in the spotlight. Not Chet's style at all.

As Chet surreptitiously studied the crowd, he noticed a few familiar faces. Cowboys like him who'd arrived in town a few days early for the rodeo. One of the cowboys, Blake Turnbull, caught his eye and nodded. Blake was a saddle bronc rider and a decent guy. They weren't exactly friends, but a few years back Blake had come to him asking for some financial advice.

Having grown up poor, with a father who spent every

paycheck the minute the cash hit the bank, Chet was determined to do the opposite. He saved the bulk of every purse, which meant he lived miserly, but the security of seeing his nest egg grow exponentially was his reward. Since he turned eighteen, he'd also spent his winters taking online college courses. Mostly about finance and taxes and practical things like that. Two years ago he'd amassed enough credits to get his Certified Financial Planning certificate.

He'd done it all out of personal interest and his need for financial security. But when word got out on the circuit that he knew a thing or two, he started to field questions from some of the guys. And Blake had been one of those guys.

His coffee arrived, nice and hot.

"Your burger will be out shortly," the server promised, retreating quickly.

Chet sipped the strong coffee and went back to observing the crowd. Some of customers looked like local ranchers. Dusty boots and honest grime clinging to their jeans gave them away. Over by the pool tables a couple of pretty ladies, all made up, long hair in curls, jeans tight and tops low-cut, were attracting their share of attention. They seemed happy to joke around with the cowboys who approached them, but turned down offers of drinks and dances.

"Hey, Chet." Blake had made his way to Chet's booth.

Chet nodded. "Blake."

Blake hesitated, maybe expecting he'd be invited to sit. But Chet didn't do that. In theory he was open to the idea of friends. And maybe even wanted some. But he was more comfortable with animals than people.

"Sorry to bother you," Blake continued. "But I just want to thank you. I've been saving, following your advice and investing carefully. I'm getting married this fall, and thanks to you, I have enough put aside for a down payment on a house."

"I'm glad to hear that. But thank yourself. You're the one who had the discipline to set aside that money. I hope you keep up the good financial habits once you're married."

"I plan to."

Chet's burger arrived then and Blake left him to eat in peace. Though he'd shrugged off any credit, Chet did feel good inside, knowing he'd helped Blake make responsible financial choices. Too many young cowboys blew the money they made on the rodeo. They exchanged their youth, their talent and their young, strong bodies for money they wasted on living high. When they did invest their money they made stupid choices—high-end trucks and expensive clothes that would have no value fifteen years down the road.

Chet's own truck was one he'd bought second-hand ten years ago. And it still worked just fine.

Chet bit into his burger, which was damn good. As he savored each bite, he studied the photographs on the wall. If he'd invited Blake to join him, he would have had someone to talk to. He could have asked about Blake's fiancée, what kind of wedding they'd be having, stuff like that.

The men and women on the rodeo circuit were a genial bunch for the most part. But though he'd lived the life since he was eight years old—first following his dad, then as an errand boy, and finally as a contestant—Chet had always felt like an outsider. Part of it was his dad's reputation as a drinker and a troublemaker. The rest was just him. He'd never figured out where he belonged. Mostly it just felt safer to stick to himself.

AMY CHECKED TWO new guests into Bramble House late that afternoon. Fred and Sue Lancaster were in their mid-forties. They'd traveled from their home in Washington State to watch their daughter compete in the barrel-racing event at the rodeo.

"Ruby Lancaster. She's only twenty, but she's doing really well this year. Have you heard of her?" Fred asked.

"I don't know much about the rodeo," Amy admitted. "But that's exciting your daughter is doing well. I've put you in the Mable Suite on the main floor. You have a private outdoor seating area outside the patio doors." She handed Fred a pen to sign the guest registry.

"We thought we'd come a few days early to do some hiking in the area," Sue told her while her husband was busy. "Do you have any recommendations?"

"I'm sorry, I'm new to the area as well. Maybe you could

try Tourist Information?" In a fit of organizing and decluttering, Amy had inadvertently relegated to recycling, along with a bunch of outdated magazines, the collection of brochures to local businesses and attractions that Eliza had kept on hand for guests. She needed to visit Tourist Information to restock. When she found the time.

Sue didn't look impressed, but she gave a nod. "Any recommendations for dinner?"

"I have heard the Graff Hotel is wonderful. Would you like me to make a reservation?"

"If it isn't too expensive. We're on a budget," Fred said.

"Hm, in that case you might want to try someplace else. I'm sure there are several options on Main Street." Amy wished she could name some of them, but so far, her only excursions had been to the local market and bakery to purchase items she needed for breakfast and afternoon tea.

Amy showed the Lancasters to their room and made sure they had enough towels, then went to restock the sideboard in the sitting room. According to the Bramble House binder, tea, coffee and sometimes lemonade or iced tea was available here from three to five in the afternoon, along with a bowl of fruit and some fresh baked goods.

Sounded easy. But in practice Amy found it annoying to have to keep the thermoses of coffee and tea fresh and it was expensive to buy baked goods. The fruit went bad if people didn't eat it, but when she put out a simple bowl of long-lived apples, she could count on someone asking if she had anything else.

Somehow her day slipped by without her having time to replace the light bulb in the hall. Amy added *buy light bulbs at hardware store* to her to-do list for the following day, then went outside to enjoy the sunset.

No matter how crazy her day, she always carved out fifteen minutes for this. She leaned back in her cushioned chair and took a deep breath. The view from her porch faced south but the glow from the sunset crept in from the west, casting streaks of peach and violet and indigo over the sky and the mountains, colors that were then reflected in the gently flowing water of the river.

Fifteen minutes of heaven. Was it enough?

Amy pushed down the feeling of panic, the fear that her friends and colleagues were right, and she had made a terrible mistake coming here. Investing all the money she had inherited—her mother's nest egg for the retirement she had not been fated to live—into a white elephant of a building and a business she seemed doomed to fail at.

She recognized her thoughts were in a negative spiral. Since the accident that had been happening a lot. Her work in finance had felt meaningless, her apartment achingly empty without her mother. Just when she'd desperately needed the release of her long-distance running, thanks to her injury, even that was lost.

Moving to Montana was supposed to be like hitting a reset button, returning her to her factory-programmed settings. Confident. Ambitious. Cheerful. Someone who worked hard and generally succeeded. Someone who liked people and who people almost always liked back.

But she was feeling none of the old Amy in Marietta. She'd gotten off on the wrong foot somehow. Or maybe she was too much of a city girl to fit into this cowboy western culture.

Seeing Chet Hardwick drive up in his dusty old Ford was a welcome diversion. She watched as he parked across the street, then got out from the cab. He reached back in for a shopping bag, then shut the door.

She would wave if he looked her way, but he didn't. She supposed she shouldn't be surprised. He'd made it clear he preferred his own company, and she got it that a B & B atmosphere wasn't for everyone. Yet behind that gruff, *I'd rather sleep in a barn* exterior of his, she'd glimpsed a kind and gentle man, not her expectation of your average cowboy. But then, what did she know of cowboys? Only what she'd gleaned from shows like *Yellowstone*. They were tough and lived by their own moral code—though that code didn't seem to set many limits. For example, murder seemed okay.

Probably not fair of her to use a highly rated TV show to judge real-life people. Hollywood and the entertainment industry weren't kind to people who worked on Wall Street like her, either. But fictional stereotypes were all she had to go on so far. Though she'd seen lots of cowboys since she'd moved here, so far she hadn't gotten to know any of them.

But if she had to start with one, she'd pick Chet Hardwick. Despite his anti B & B attitude he'd made a good impression. Starting with those warm brown eyes of his.

Though he was a good-looking man, apparently single, not much older than her, he hadn't given her the bold ogle of a guy on the make, or the dismissive glance of someone whose thoughts were primarily on himself. No, Chet had made thoughtful eye contact. She appreciated that he hadn't tried to argue his way out of her cancellation policy, even though he'd obviously been unhappy about it. And he'd been kind to worry about her finger and sacrifice one of his grandmother's cotton handkerchiefs to the cause.

Thinking of the handkerchief reminded her that she needed to return it. After a long, soapy, cold-water presoak and a hot-water wash with a whitening agent, it had finally come clean. She'd even pressed it into a neat square—the way it had looked when he'd first pulled it from his pocket.

Before he reached the stairs to his above-the-garage retreat, she called out, "I've washed your handkerchief if you'd like it back."

He hesitated, then turned her way. He tipped his hat as he grew near, an acknowledgment by way of hello. Any other man she'd known would have looked ridiculous in that hat. But on Chet it looked totally natural. And rather hot.

She slipped inside to retrieve the handkerchief and then handed it to him. "How are your horses?"

"Doing fine, thank you." He held up the paper bag in his

hand. "Brought some bulbs. Thought I'd replace the burnt-out one in the morning."

She didn't understand at first. Then she noticed the logo on the bag: *Big Z Hardware*. He was referring to the light bulb she needed in the hallway. "I meant to buy some this afternoon but forgot. How kind of you to bother with that."

"Not a problem. I needed to get some other stuff anyway. I can take care of it right now if you like."

"No thanks. You're a guest," she insisted. She held out a hand for the bag and finally he passed it over. "Is the receipt in here? I'll get my wallet and pay you back."

"No rush. Sit down and enjoy the view. It sure is a beautiful sunset tonight."

She felt she ought to argue, but this was her fifteen minutes and she deserved to enjoy every one of them. "It really is. And these are great seats to appreciate it from. Feel free to join me," she said, indicating the chair next to hers.

She fully expected him to make an excuse and leave. But he didn't. He took a seat and removed his hat, setting it top side down on the wide porch railing. As he combed his fingers through his hair, she admired the thick, dark waves. He had neat ears, and a nice nose, though there was a bump at the bridge. Perhaps he'd broken it at some point.

She glanced away, aware she was staring.

"So how did your day go?" he finally asked her.

"The usual madness. Laundry and cleaning, of course. Then I paid some bills, restocked supplies, checked in some new guests and managed to water the flowers on the porch."

He took a look around. "They look happier than they did this afternoon."

"Yes." But the grass still needed cutting, the laundry folding and she still hadn't prepped breakfast for tomorrow morning. Amy took another deep breath and tried to focus on the view. The beautiful sunset. Not the man.

"Did you get a chance to bake those cookies?" he asked.

"I tried." She sighed. "But they didn't work out, so I bought some in town, as well as chocolates for the turndown service."

"Turndown service? I hope you didn't bother with my room."

"Nope. I kept to our deal. I won't step inside your room unless you ask me to." Oh, darn, that came out wrong. "Like if you need towels or something," she added quickly.

Chet looked amused. "One towel will do me fine. Not that I want you to feel unwelcome in my room."

Was he flirting? His tone was so deadpan. But there had been a momentary glint in his eye. She decided to deflect by offering him one of the milk chocolate boots she'd brought out with her.

"Is this from Sage's shop?"

She nodded.

"Don't mind if I do then."

They both took their time eating the chocolate, silently watching as twilight descended and the pastels in the sky merged and deepened to a rich sapphire blue.

The color reminded Amy of the stones in her bracelet and her conversation with Portia. Though she'd been polite, it was clear Portia and her family thought Amy was doing a bad job at the B & B. They probably thought she was going to fail. Maybe they even wanted her to?

"Well, I'll have to show them, won't I?" Who needed a staff? With her time management and operations skills she'd soon work out a schedule that she could handle on her own.

She didn't realize she'd spoken any of this aloud until Chet said, "Show them what?"

With a weary shrug she said, "Oh, the people in this town. They've already judged me and found me below par I'm afraid."

He gazed at her thoughtfully, but didn't say anything.

Sunset was over, along with her fifteen minutes of downtime. She ought to go inside and chop veggies for the frittata she'd be making in the morning. But it was nice sitting here with Chet. The man was intriguing, and she wanted to know him better. At the same time she could tell she needed to be judicious with her questions.

"What made you decide to be a rodeo cowboy?"

He gave a short laugh. "There was no deciding about it. I was born into the lifestyle. My father was a bull rider. After my grandmother died, I lived with him full time and I picked up things. I tried a little of everything but finally settled on tie-down roping as my event."

"I hate to sound ignorant, but what is that exactly?"

He looked a little surprised, a little amused. "You didn't do much research before moving here, did you? Basically a calf gets a head start running into the rodeo ring, then I follow and lasso him, flank him, and tie three of his legs together. The idea is to do all this fast. It's a timed event."

"Do you enjoy it?"

"I love my horses. I have fun roping. But the competing can get intense. The pressure gets to you after a while."

"Do you worry about hurting the calves?"

"You ever been on a working cattle ranch?" Chet asked her.

"No."

"Well, roping calves is part of the job for a ranch hand. And it doesn't hurt the calves. They're a lot tougher than they look."

She wasn't sure she believed that. "Have you worked on a cattle ranch, too?"

"Sure. During off-season I'm a ranch hand for a big operation in Colorado. Not many people make a full-time living from rodeo."

"What do you make of the argument that cattle ranching is bad for the environment?"

He gave her a long, searching look. "A lot of things are bad for the environment. Take iron-ore smelting. Every ton of steel produced releases almost double that amount of carbon dioxide into the atmosphere. Do people say we need to give up steel? No, they say we need to find a smarter way to make steel. Same goes for cattle ranching. Lots of people are working on smarter, more sustainable ranching practices."

"What you say makes sense. But you can't deny that the footprint of beef is a lot greater than the footprint of producing legumes, for instance."

"Taking private jets is awful for the environment. But we haven't outlawed them." He cocked his head at her. "You don't like cattle ranching, you don't like rodeo. Why did you leave New York City to move to Montana?"

She turned her gaze away, toward the mountains that were now just hulking dark shapes against the navy sky. "There is more to Montana than rodeos and cattle ranching."

"Yeah. But they're a big part of the lifestyle and the heritage."

"That may be true. But I don't have to like them."

Chet settled his hat back on his head and rose slowly from his chair. "You think the people in this town are judging you, Amy. Aren't you doing the same to them?"

Chapter Four

CHET'S PARTING WORDS stayed with Amy as she finished her chores for the night, and they were the first thing she thought about when she woke at six the next morning. He hadn't given her a chance to respond or defend her position. But even if he had, she wasn't sure what she would have said.

Because it was possible he was right. That she'd leapt to judgments about the people of this town just the way they seemed to be doing to her.

A humbling realization.

In the kitchen she paused for a moment, savoring a few seconds of tranquility before the hustle and bustle of her day began. This was her favorite room in Bramble House. The kitchen was old-fashioned, with butcher-block countertops, an original farm-style sink, and lots of open shelves housing gallon-sized glass jars containing oats, lentils, beans, cornmeal and other staples. The flour was stored in a six-gallon, pull-out bin and the deep windowsills were filled with pots of commonly used herbs like basil, mint, oregano and chives.

After putting on the first pot of coffee, Amy pulled the

large pan of chopped veggies and grated cheese from the fridge, then the bowl of mixed eggs and cream. After giving the egg mixture a thorough whisking, she poured it over the veggies and cheese. A sprinkle of chopped fresh basil on top and it was ready to go into the preheated oven.

She stopped for a moment to pat herself on the back. Neither she nor her mother had much interest in cooking beyond the basics. There were so many excellent restaurants and takeout options in New York. But while it was satisfying to have mastered a new recipe like the frittata, it only made her more frustrated that she couldn't seem to bake a basic batch of chocolate chip cookies—something her mother had taught her when she was ten.

Since then, she'd baked hundreds of batches of cookies. They were her go-to snack when she was studying for midterms or finals.

She must be doing something wrong…but what? Thank goodness Eliza had left dozens of blueberry bran muffins and several loaves of banana and pumpkin loaf in the freezer. But soon those would be gone, and she was going to have to learn to bake those too.

Amy put out coffee and some thawed baked goods on the dining room sideboard for early risers, then went outside with Chet's promised thermos and muffins. It was another perfect late summer day in Marietta.

Amy's intention was to leave Chet's breakfast at his door without bothering him, but she caught him on the landing, buttoning his shirt, on his way to the truck. She paused at the foot of the stairs, admiring his lean, muscled physique, the glimpse of chest before he tackled that final button.

"Good morning," he said. "And good timing. Can I take that thermos with me?"

"Sure. Just drop it off in the kitchen before tomorrow morning."

"No problem." He came down the stairs at a trot, but rather than hand over the coffee and bag of muffins she walked with him toward his truck.

"You were right yesterday when you said it wasn't fair of me to judge the Montana lifestyle."

"Yeah, well some of that was me being defensive. You've a right to your opinion."

"But it should be an educated one. I've been so busy I haven't had a chance to meet new people or get out and explore." Then again, the people of this town hadn't fallen over themselves to welcome her either. Except for a middle-aged woman named Carol Bingley who had stopped by on Amy's moving day with a casserole.

Carol and her husband owned the local pharmacy and they lived on her block. Yet despite the hospitable gesture, Amy didn't think she and Carol were destined to be friends. The woman had asked too many questions, going beyond friendly to prying. And then she'd provided gossip about some of their mutual neighbors that had made Amy feel uncomfortable.

"Have you considered hiring new help?" Chet asked. "Though it might be difficult to find someone in the middle of the summer—especially the week before the rodeo," he conceded.

"It's a lot of work on my own," she admitted. "But at least this way I'm learning all the aspects of my new business firsthand. There's value in that."

"There's also value in having a few hours off every day." They'd reached his truck, and Chet took the thermos and bag from her hands. He put the muffins on the passenger seat, then opened the thermos and took a sip.

"Ah. Good coffee."

"It wasn't made in a barn, but I'm glad it passes muster."

He grinned. "Something tells me you're not going to let me live that one down."

"And you'd be right on that."

"And you're evading the question." He raised an eyebrow. "Hiring new staff?"

"I need to," she admitted. "But I don't want just anyone. I have to find the right person. And that will take time. Maybe after rodeo week when bookings slow down."

"That makes sense."

With one hand on the open truck door, Chet took another drink of coffee. He seemed in no hurry to leave and though she had breakfast to get on the table, Amy wasn't either. She leaned against the sun-warmed metal of his truck and gazed out at the view. "Does it ever rain in Montana? Or even get cloudy? I swear the sky has been perfectly blue every day since I moved here."

"Summers tend to be hot and dry in Montana. But things will start to get interesting in October. They get some wicked storms. Rain, wind, snow, you're going to see it all." He glanced at her hand. "How's the finger?"

"Fine." She'd replaced the bandage after her shower and hadn't thought of it since. "Thanks again for removing that piece of glass."

"It was my pleasure. You sure you don't want me to replace that light bulb? I could do it now before I head out to the ranch."

"No, that's fine. I'll take care of it." He was still looking at her. Not at her finger this time. At her.

"What did you do for fun in New York? To relax?"

She sighed ruefully. "Before the accident where I injured my leg, I was a long-distance runner. And boy do I miss it."

She was wearing a skirt today and his gaze went to the scar at her knee. "What happened?"

She turned her gaze away, but she wasn't seeing the river, the mountains or the sky. She was driving north on the I-95 with her mother, watching in shock as a half-ton truck cut in front of her, hearing the explosion of metal crushing against metal, feeling the searing pain in her leg, the push of the air bag against her chest. "Car crash."

"I'm sorry. It must have been a bad one. Is the damage to your leg permanent?"

She nodded. "Yes, but that's not the worst of it. My mother was in the car with me…she didn't survive."

He rubbed the side of his face. "Man, that's rough. I'm really sorry."

The words were simple but when she raised her gaze to meet his, she was overwhelmed by the depth of compassion she saw in his rich brown eyes.

"We were driving up to the Catskills for the weekend when a truck turned off a side road, right in front of us. He had a stop sign, but I guess he didn't see us. I hit him with the right side of my car, going full highway speed." Why was she telling him this? She hadn't spoken of the accident since those awful weeks after it happened. Every time the memories flashed into her brain, she did her best to squash them.

"You were behind the wheel?"

"Yes."

"Sounds like there was nothing you could do. It was one of those horrible things. A moment of carelessness on the truck driver's part—and then tragedy."

"That's what the police who investigated the accident told me, too. It's hard not to feel guilty, though."

"You think your mother would want to saddle you with that? On top of the grief you're already suffering?"

"No, she wouldn't."

"Humans are strange creatures. Animals don't feel guilty when something bad happens to one of their pack. Sad yes, guilty no."

She smiled at the comparison. He was being silly, lightening her mood. But he did have a point.

"The accident happened over a year ago. They say the first year is the hardest. But to be honest, so far year two hasn't been much easier."

"Yeah, well my grandmother died when I was eight and I still miss her. She raised me after my own mom—her daughter—died when I was born."

"I'm sorry." Now she was the one saying the simple words. But often simple words were the best, weren't they? At least they were when they were genuine. "What was life like with your grandmother?"

"It was great. Simple, but great. She didn't have much money. We lived in a small house in Yuma. Looking back I can see it was kind of run-down, but she kept it real clean and tidy. She insisted on good manners, and I had a list of daily chores, more it seemed to me at the time, than other kids my age. But she was kind and she liked to laugh and she sure was a good cook."

"She sounds like a special woman."

"I can't imagine what it was like for her. Losing her daughter and then being handed a newborn baby to look after. At her age she'd probably been hoping to slow down. But she just smiled and did what needed to be done."

"Did your father visit you very often?"

"A couple times a year. He'd come down for the rodeo. Or stop by around Christmastime. My grandma didn't have much time for him, and I didn't look forward to his visits either. He'd take me out for a movie and then for burgers. But we had nothing to talk about. From things I overheard my grandmother say, I don't think he contributed much financially to my upbringing either."

"It must have been a rude shock for you when your grandmother passed."

"It was a rude shock for my old man too, I suppose." He looked out at the mountains then back at her. "I can't believe I'm gabbing on like this."

"Me too. I guess I've been feeling more lonely than I admitted. And you're a good listener."

"You'll make friends here in time," Chet predicted. "In the meantime you need to find something to replace running in your life."

"My best girlfriend from college suggested swimming. But it's not the same. I love being outside, feeling the breeze in my hair, the wonderful sense of freedom."

"That's the way I feel when I'm riding a horse. You ever thought of giving that a try?"

"No." Her answer came out vehemently, as if the suggestion was absurd. Which it technically wasn't. "I have no experience with horses," she added, by way of explanation.

"No experience required if you pick the right horse. And the right teacher."

"And where would I find those?"

He raised his eyebrows. "I've taught a fair number of

people to ride in my time. Most of them kids, but the principles are the same. I wouldn't put a novice on one of my horses, but I could ask at the Circle C. I'm sure they have a gentle mount who could use some exercise."

Even though she was intrigued by the opportunity to get to know Chet better, something inside of Amy resisted. She felt her stomach tighten, her heart race. It was fear, she realized. She was afraid of hurting herself again.

"That's okay. Like I said, I really don't have the time."

"If you say so." Chet opened the truck door wider. "I better get going. My horses are going to be feeling neglected."

"Right." She stepped away from the truck. "And I need to serve my guests some breakfast. They're not all low maintenance like you."

Chet smiled at that as he settled into his seat. Before shutting the door though, he had some parting words. "If you want to give the Montana lifestyle a fair shake, learning to ride a horse might be a good place to start."

THE RIDING LESSONS were in the back of Amy's mind as she hurried through her morning routine. Yes, she was afraid, but if she had a gentle horse it wouldn't be too dangerous would it? She did like the idea of being able to explore the beautiful countryside. And Chet made a good point about trying to fit in. If she ended up enjoying the sport, it might be a way to meet new people.

All of this was moot at the moment, however, since she simply couldn't carve enough time from her day to give it a try. Her to-do list just for today was formidable and breakfast was the most hectic time.

Amy was slicing the frittata when her doc crew guests came downstairs. The three of them had arrived on Sunday with plans to stay until after rodeo finals the following Sunday. She'd put them in the Blue, Brown and Red rooms on the second floor. Really, the naming of those rooms after colors was just so boring. Yet the way Jo and Ella had gasped when she'd suggested naming them after nearby national parks—Glacier, Yellowstone and Grand Teton—you'd think she was trying to rewrite the Bible.

"Good morning," Amy greeted them. "I have your green tea, Lucy, an Americano for Graham and diet cola for Rick." What had happened to people simply having coffee in the morning? Amy wondered. It would make life so much easier.

The three of them chose seats around the table. There was no conversation as Rick and Graham focused on their phones while Amy made edits to a list on her clipboard.

They were working on a documentary about the western rodeo tradition, focusing on five small towns, including Marietta. Lucy Wilson was the producer, close to Amy's age with sleek honey-colored hair and a sharp, inquisitive mind. Her go-to summer wardrobe ran to sleeveless dresses and wedge sandals and she always looked cool and put-together.

Graham North, blond and handsome, charming and smooth, spoke with a silky baritone, and conducted all the interviews for the documentary.

In contrast to the polished Lucy and Graham was Rick Johnson, the videographer. Though he was thirty, he looked like the kind of guy who had never stopped living with his parents. His dark hair could really use a good wash and a brushing, and he dressed in baggy cargo shorts and T-shirts that managed to be too wide while also being too short.

"So what are you up to today?" Amy asked as she served plates of frittata, fruit salad and local pork sausages.

"More local color," Lucy said, not elaborating.

Yesterday, their first morning at Bramble House, she had been full of questions for Amy. "We like staying at bed-and-breakfasts because we always get the inside scoop."

But Amy had no inside scoop on Marietta, and the team had now deemed her of little interest.

Amy was clearing plates and her guests were on their second round of morning beverages, when the chime at the front door sounded and a deep male voice called out, "Hello. Anyone home?"

Amy hurried from the dining room to the front hall. Standing at the open door was a broad-shouldered cowboy and a slender woman with long strawberry-blonde hair. "Hi, I'm Amy. Can I help you?"

"We're here to see the film crew from Seattle," the cowboy said. "I'm Jake Richards and this is my fiancée Willow McBride."

Willow, who had been craning her neck to get a look at the sitting room to her right and the library to her left, finally turned her gaze to Amy. "Nice to meet you. I've always loved Bramble House. Any chance I could get a quick tour?"

Amy knew the library needed dusting and vacuuming and she still hadn't cleaned up from yesterday's afternoon tea in the sitting room. "Maybe another day," she said vaguely. "Right now why don't you make yourself comfortable on the front porch and I'll let Lucy, Graham and Rick know you're here." She stepped forward, ushering the couple outside, then closed the door firmly and went back to the dining room.

"Some people are here to see you," she told the crew. "Jake Richards and Willow McBride?"

"Great." Lucy turned to Graham. "This is the rodeo couple I was telling you about. They're getting married on Thursday and then competing in the rodeo on the weekend."

"Awesome. Just the human-interest story we need." Graham sprang up from his chair while Rick gathered the equipment he'd brought down with him.

No sooner had they left than the Lancasters showed up dressed in hiking shorts and merino wool T-shirts. Sue Lancaster's shirt said, *Hike More, Worry Less*. Amy supposed there was no point in reminding them that breakfast was supposed to be over fifteen minutes ago. Her fluffy, golden frittata would now be sunken and rubbery.

"Good morning. Would you like coffee?"

"Yes, thanks," Fred said. "Something sure smells good. What's for breakfast?"

When Amy told them, Fred wrinkled his nose. "Frittata? What's that, some sort of quiche?"

Leaving Sue to do the explaining, Amy went back to the kitchen to get their plates. "It was better fresh out of the oven at eight," she admitted.

"Maybe tomorrow you could just fry us some eggs?" Fred said, jabbing his fork into the eggs.

"We were wondering if you provide packed lunches?" Sue asked. "We're doing a hike to some waterfalls today. We got a map from Tourist Information."

Packed lunches. Amy vaguely remembered reading something about that in the Bramble binder. "Um, not this week, I'm sorry."

Sue waved her hand. "Never mind. We'll pick up something at the Main Street Diner. We went there for dinner last night and the prices were quite reasonable."

It was past ten by the time the Lancasters left the dining room. Amy cleaned the kitchen, threw in a load of laundry, did a quick dust and vacuum of the foyer and sitting room, then went outside to tackle mowing the lawn.

As she pushed the mower along the flower beds she could see there were a lot more weeds than she'd realized. Some, like the dandelions and thistles, she would be confident to pull out. But she had no clue about most of them. Living in apartments all her life she knew precious little about gardening. Somehow she was going to have to make the time to learn.

Amy had made her way through half the front lawn when a couple drove up in a car with Alberta plates. They parked across the street, pausing to admire the view before heading toward her.

The man and woman looked to be in their early sixties, dressed in casual western wear. Already Amy could spot the difference between the way the rodeo tourists dressed versus the cowboys. These were obviously tourists.

Amy shut off the motor on the lawn mower and removed her working gloves, tucking one each into the back pockets of her jeans.

The man, medium height with gray hair and a deep tan, gave her a smile. "Hi, we're the Murphys from Calgary. I know this is a long shot but do you by chance have a room available? We had booked into a guest ranch in Paradise Valley, but they had a plumbing issue and our room is out of commission."

Thanks to Chet taking the room over the garage, she did. "You're in luck. I do have one room on the second story with a queen bed and en suite bath. Would you like to see it?"

"I'm sure it's fine. We'll take it. Is it too early to check in? Should we ask inside?"

It was only noon and check-in time was officially four, but Amy waved him forward. "It's a team of one around here at the moment, so I'll check you in. And as it happens your room is ready so you're welcome now."

"Okay, we'll grab our suitcases and be right with you."

Amy took the time to put away her gloves and wash her hands before joining them in the foyer. They were studying the old family photos on the wall, the ones she hoped to eventually replace with pictures of Paradise Valley and nearby Yellowstone Park.

"Is this your family, dear?" the woman asked, peering at a faded black-and-white photo of the original Bramble family.

"No. I recently purchased this place from the Brambles. They made their money mining copper, I believe, and built this place in the 1880s."

"What a shame they had to let it go. I hope you'll keep up the history. These old homes are such treasures."

They signed in to the register as Penny and Dusty Murphy. And once she'd shown them to the White room—which they seemed very happy with, though they did ask for more towels—they pulled out this year's Copper Mountain Rodeo program.

"We've been to a lot of rodeos in Alberta and Montana," Dusty said. "This is the first time we've made it this far south. Thought we'd arrive early and soak up some of the atmosphere. Any suggestions what we should do?"

Mentally Amy groaned. She really did need to bone up

on the local tourist sites and attractions. Or at least pick up an assortment of brochures. "I'm new around here. But you can't go wrong starting with Main Street. There are so many interesting shops and delicious eateries. And the historic Graff Hotel is not to be missed. I definitely recommend you make a dinner reservation for at least one night of your stay."

"I wonder if we can get in tonight?" Penny said.

"I could phone and check for you," Amy offered. "Any preferred time?"

"Around six would be perfect." Penny gave her a grateful smile. Her husband was still flipping through the program, checking out the ads from local businesses. He pointed at one. "This Main Street Diner looks like a good place for lunch."

"I've heard their prices are good," Amy said.

Penny clapped her hands. "Perfect. I just need my sunglasses. Sweetheart, did you see where I put them?"

Amy left the couple, returning to the front desk where she was able to get the Murphys a six o'clock reservation at the Graff. She wrote a note, including the Graff address and phone number and was about to take it up to their room, when she heard the couple coming down the stairs.

Penny waved her sunglasses. "Found them!"

"Good, you'll definitely need them. I haven't lived in Montana for long, but it is definitely the sunniest place I've ever been." She passed Dusty the note with their reservation information.

"Thank you. Just a few more questions before we head out?" Dusty said.

"Sure. I'll try to help, though like I said, I'm new here too."

While her husband asked Amy about gas stations, tourist information sites and good places for hiking, Penny perused the old family photos. Finally, about fifteen minutes later, the couple were on their way.

Amy took the extra towels to their room before she forgot. When she returned to the front desk where she'd stowed her work gloves, she saw the Murphys had forgotten their rodeo program. She ran outside with it, but they were already gone.

She glanced at the half-mowed lawn, but after a rumble from her stomach, decided she'd better grab a quick sandwich before she finished the job. She took the program with her, leafing through the pages as she munched through a hummus, herbed cream cheese and cucumber sandwich.

There was a message from the rodeo committee on the first page of the program, and another from the town's mayor Chelsea Collier Flint. Lots of ads from local businesses followed—including one for Bramble House, which Eliza must have purchased back when she was running the place.

Amy read an article about how the rodeo grounds were rebuilt after a fire in 2020 and then she came to the program of events.

The weekend kicked off Friday night with a barbecue

and street dancing on Main Street. Saturday morning there was a parade from Main Street to the fairgrounds. This year they were honoring Montana cowboy hall-of-famers, and here there was a list of names, which Amy skipped.

She was more interested in the rodeo itself, which started Saturday at one o'clock. Amy skimmed past the opening events to the tie-down roping event. She scanned the list of contestants, until she spotted Chet's name. He was the fifth contestant out of ten. At the back section of the program she found a brief bio.

Chet Hardwick
Tie-down roping, 11th world standing in 2022
Born in Denver, Colorado
Joined PRCA in 2014
Won the RAM Texas Circuit Finals Rodeo (Waco)
Won New Mexico State Fair & Rodeo Albuquerque
Won the all-around at Livingston Montana Roundup
Won the Snake River Stampede (Nampa, Idaho)

It looked like an impressive list of accomplishments to Amy. She couldn't help but think how different his life had been to hers. All the places he'd gone to visit and compete. She'd lived her entire life in her mother's apartment in New York City—except when she'd been in college—keeping a razer focus on education and finance and her Wall Street job, with only her long-distance running as an outlet.

She went through the rest of the program, more closely this time, looking for other names that might be familiar. But nothing stood out until she came upon the list of local rodeo hall-of-famers. This time a name jumped out at her: David Wilcox.

The same name as her father.

Amy flipped pages until she found his biographical information—he'd been inducted to the hall of fame in 2021 and currently resided in Gardiner, Montana, with his wife, artist Mary Beth Wilcox, and their three sons.

Amy fingered her silver bracelet, sliding it up and down her arm.

Weeks after her mother had died, Amy had finally worked up the courage to go through the things in her mother's bedroom. She'd found no surprises until she came to her mother's bedside table. Inside one of the drawers she'd found the box for her mother's silver bracelet. Stamped on the bottom of the box had been: *J. P. & Sons Jewelers, Limited, Marietta, Montana.*

Under the box had been a two-page, handwritten love letter to her mom. There had been no envelope, no forwarding address. Amy guessed the letter had been hand-delivered. As she read it, the details meshed exactly with the little her mother had told her over a decade ago, when she'd asked about her father.

Amy had always known the bracelet had been a gift to her mom from her father. She also knew the story about how the two of them had met, on the first day of her mother's camping holiday in Yellowstone Park. Her mother had gone with a group of girlfriends but after meeting this guy she'd ditched her friends and spent the rest of her holiday with him.

Months later, back in New York, when Amy's mom realized she was pregnant, she'd tried to reach the guy by snail mail, but he'd never replied. These were the days before everyone had a portable phone, but Amy's mother admitted she could have tried harder to track him down, perhaps hired an investigator. But like her, he was only nineteen years old. She barely knew him, didn't want to marry him, and even if she did, she was committed to New York and he to Montana.

In the end, she opted to have and raise the baby—Amy—on her own.

At that point her mom had asked Amy if she wanted to meet her father. If so, she would help her find him. But Amy had not felt the need. Her life was busy and fulfilling and she had her mom.

But that had been then.

After the accident, after her mother was gone and nothing felt right anymore, Amy found herself fixating on her father. She tried searching him out on the internet, but he had a very common name, and she found several possibilities in Montana alone. And it was always conceivable he had moved.

But perhaps more likely that he hadn't.

She tried focusing her search on the town where he'd purchased her mother's bracelet: Marietta. When she discovered Marietta was only a few hours from Yellowstone National Park, she realized she was on to something.

It was during those days of searching the internet that Amy had encountered the real estate listing for Bramble House Bed-and-Breakfast.

She couldn't pinpoint the moment she got the idea to buy the place. All she knew was she was ready for a change. She needed to get away from the city, where every turn brought with it an aching memory of her mom.

Also, her curiosity about her father was growing. What kind of man was he? What parts of her did she owe to him, to his genes, his DNA?

Her plan had been to track him down once she moved here. And, if he was still alive, to meet him. So far she hadn't found the time. Now it seemed she may not need to. David Wilcox was coming to her.

Chapter Five

CHET DIDN'T KNOW why Amy's predicament was weighing on him. It wasn't like him to stick his nose in other people's business.

It bothered him that she was new to town, a rookie at the B & B business, and all her staff had deserted her. He could relate to the feeling of being an outsider. He'd felt that way most of his life.

All the other kids in the various schools he'd attended had seemed to have two parents, even if they didn't live in the same house. The few that had just one parent usually had a mom. But his had died during childbirth. Chet knew that wasn't his fault. But his father had always made him feel it was.

Wish they could have saved my wife rather than the baby.

He'd heard his father say those words more than once. Maybe his father hadn't intended him to hear. More likely he hadn't cared one way or the other. Chet couldn't remember his father ever showing him any genuine sign of affection.

Sometimes he wondered what his father would have been

like if his mother had lived. Would he have been a happier, kinder man? Would he have been less of a drinker, maybe held down a regular job, lived in the same town for more than a few months at a time?

He knew his grandmother's opinion. She'd openly disliked Walt and bitterly rued the day he'd married her daughter. This made Chet suspect that his mother's death hadn't turned Walt into a mean, dishonest drunk but merely hastened the process.

What Chet really didn't understand was why his father hadn't given him up as a ward of the state, since clearly his existence had been nothing but a bother and a burden to the man. Most likely his grandmother's estate had something to do with it. She'd left her home and meagre savings to her grandson and since Chet was underage, that meant Walt had control of it.

He'd sold the house and what he did with the money Chet never knew. He guessed Walt had paid off old debts. Certainly Walt never used the money to rent a decent home for the two of them, or to buy clothing or school supplies for Chet. Those were things Chet learned to scrounge for young, at thrift shops. He also collected bottles and took them to the depot to get money for the things he couldn't find at second-hand stores, things like pencils and pens and notebooks for school.

The day Chet turned sixteen had been a relief to both of them. Though he wasn't of official legal age, Chet was old enough to drive and old enough to work. He got a job on a ranch that provided room and board. Hit the local rodeos. Saved to buy his first horse.

After that the only times he saw the old man were when they accidently attended the same rodeo. Something they both tried to avoid.

It was after one when Chet left the Circle C ranch, horses exercised, fed and groomed. He drove into town and grabbed a sandwich and coffee at the Java Café, then sat on a bench outside to eat.

Chet had seen a lot of small towns in his life, and Marietta had to be one of the prettiest. Lots of trees and planters brimming with flowers. The storefronts were well maintained and right now, most had displays supporting the upcoming rodeo, including Sage's chocolate shop, across the street.

Not all rodeo cowgirls and cowboys transitioned easily out of the life, but Sage and Dawson had. She had her successful business and Dawson worked as a deputy. Between them they had two kids and a beautiful house just down the street from Bramble House.

He hoped his own transition from rodeo life would go as well.

At thirty he still had a few more years in him, at least physically, but mentally he was tired of the nomadic lifestyle and the pressure of competing. He wanted to settle down, buy a house, get a regular job. But a big part of him was scared to take that leap. Rodeo was all he knew. What if he put down roots and they didn't take? Not all transplanted things flourished.

He was just finishing his sandwich and thinking of moving on, when Sage came out of her shop. He didn't know how she normally dressed for work, but today she was going full-on rodeo in jeans, proper boots, and a western shirt. The look suited her. It always had.

She waved at him, then crossed the street.

"I thought it was you." She sat next to him on the bench, and then passed him a milk chocolate cowboy boot. "Want some dessert?"

"If it's your chocolate, always." He ate the treat fast so it wouldn't melt in the midday heat.

"So are your horses happy out at the Circle C?"

"Yeah, they're doing great. That's a beautiful property your family owns."

"Right? I'm grateful Callan and Court are making it possible for us to keep it in the family. Our family is getting bigger and spreading out, but we still gather back at the ranch at least two times a year—Christmas and rodeo week."

"Was it hard seeing Bramble House pass out of the hands of family?"

"Yes. But realistically we had to sell. Eliza and Marshall were doing a wonderful job with it, but Marshall's heart was always hankering for adventure. They just took on a year's contract to run a backcountry lodge in Colorado. Helicopter access, very remote. It would scare me silly to live in a place like that during winter, but they're thrilled."

"I take it they don't have kids?"

"Actually they have twin boys. Eliza plans to homeschool them for the year."

"Do they know their staff quit on Amy's first day?"

Sage looked surprised by the question. "I'm not sure. They weren't here for the closing, they were already up at the lodge. I know Eliza felt badly that she wasn't able to meet Amy, but she put together a wonderful binder on Bramble House including all her favorite recipes."

"I'm just asking because I assume Eliza—and the rest of your family—want the B & B to be a success? If Amy can't make a go of it, she'll probably have to sell. And who knows what the next owner might do to the place."

Sage studied his face for a long moment. "Sounds like you've gotten pretty invested in Bramble House already. Or is it Amy?"

"Just making an observation." Sage was right, he was invested—heaven only knew why—but he would never admit it. "It's a tough business for a novice without any staff to help her. Not that Amy will admit it. She's determined to do it all on her own. Wouldn't even let me change a light bulb for her."

Sage looked troubled. "I should have stopped in to welcome her when she first arrived, but we were so busy with rodeo week approaching and then Dawson's mother announced she was coming to visit. I admit it's not easy to see a stranger in my mother's old home. Bramble House was a fixture for our family."

"Any idea why the staff quit?"

"Well, Jo and Ella both came to me the day they resigned," she admitted. "Their feathers were ruffled because Amy wanted to shake things up. I should have tried harder to convince them to give Amy a chance."

"Did you try at all?"

"Not really. No," she admitted. Then she sighed. "Point taken, Chet. Our family—and myself in particular—should be supporting Amy, not leaving her to fend on her own. I promise to go over and introduce myself in the next day or two. And I'll talk to Ella and Jo as well."

SEEING HER FATHER'S name in the rodeo program made Amy impatient to find out if he was indeed the David Wilcox her mother had told her about. Now that she knew his occupation and hometown, as well as his name, she went back online and had more success tracking him down to a Facebook page. She stared at his profile picture for a long time. He was a big, broad-shouldered man with a friendly, weathered face, bright eyes—blue like hers—and a humorous twist to his mouth. His hair, though streaked with gray, looked like it had once been blond.

She wouldn't say she looked like him—in size and features she favored her mother—but there were similarities. The fair hair and blue eyes, and something about his smile… Her gut told her this was indeed her father.

She poised the cursor over the Add Friend button. Then the Message option. All she had to do was reach out. Within this very day she could probably confirm that he was indeed the man who had met Helen Arden in the summer of 1997.

She tried to imagine his reaction if she sent him a message. Did he even know she existed? Maybe her mother's letter about the pregnancy had gone astray. Or maybe, despite all the coincidences, he wasn't the David Wilcox her mother had met.

Amy tried to work up the nerve to compose the first message to begin their conversation.

But she couldn't.

Instead, she decided to check out the jewelry store where her mother's bracelet had been purchased. Maybe that would help her make sure she was on the right track. She slipped her bracelet off her wrist and returned it to the box, which she then placed into her messenger-bag-styled purse.

She felt guilty as she walked past the sitting room in need of fresh fruit and cookies, and even worse as she crossed the half-mown lawn, but she'd been in town for three weeks now without making the least effort to find her father.

It was time.

At the park she turned onto First Street and in four short

blocks she was on Front Avenue. J. P. & Sons, Montana Jewelers, was on the second floor, above the bridal store. Amy paused to admire the beautiful gown in the front window, then went up the old, narrow stairs. The stairs ended on a small landing in front of an old wooden door with a frosted window. A small sign invited her to press the buzzer for admittance, but the squeaky stairs had already announced her presence and an older gentleman pulled open the door.

"Good afternoon," he said. "Please come in."

She guessed he was in his sixties. Or possibly seventies. He was bald with stooped shoulders and wore a Mr. Rogers-style cardigan, even though the day was warm and this second-story room even warmer.

"Hi. I've come to ask you about a bracelet. It used to belong to my mother. She kept it in this box so I'm assuming it came from your shop." She took the box out of her bag and placed it on the counter.

As the jeweler reached for it, she glanced around. The shop was fitted with antique oak display cabinets and an old-fashioned cash register on the far counter. There were framed black-and-white photos on the wall of what appeared to be a mine, mineral samples, and men at work crafting jewelry. The whole process.

She wondered how many sons of the original J. P. had worked here. And was there a younger son in the wings ready to take over when this man retired? She guessed not, since he looked well past retirement age already.

As she was taking her measure of the shop, the older man had removed the bracelet from its cushioned nest and taken it to a desk where he switched on a bright light. Using a fancy-looking magnifying lens he examined it closely.

"As I thought, this is one of my designs. I need to check my records but I believe it dates back to the late 1990s. I've made a lot of similar bracelets over the years. I like to modify the design of each bracelet slightly, so the customer owns a unique piece."

"It's a beautiful bracelet. My mother wore it every day." *Like a wedding band.* The comparison slid into her thoughts out of nowhere. And yet it was apt. Over the years her mother had accumulated many beautiful pieces of jewelry. Yet this was the only piece she had never gone without.

"Did you have a question about the bracelet?" the jeweler asked. "I can tell you it's made of 92.5 percent sterling silver and the stones are Montana sapphires. Do you want to sell it? Is that why you're here? I'm afraid it's not particularly valuable. The ones I make now go for two hundred dollars."

"No," she said quickly. "I don't want to sell it. I was just curious. It obviously meant a lot to my mother. I lost her a year ago in an accident. So now it means a lot to me, too."

"I'm sorry I can't tell you anything more about it. I keep records of who buys my more expensive, custom-made pieces. But not for something like this."

"Do you sell your jewelry anywhere else? Besides this

store?"

"No. This bracelet was originally purchased here. In this very store. Of that I am certain."

"Okay. Well thank you." She held out her hand and he passed her back her bracelet. This time, instead of returning it to the box, she slipped it on her wrist.

Two hundred dollars was not a big investment when it came to jewelry. But twenty-six years ago, it would have been a considerable amount for a nineteen-year-old man, to pay for a gift for a woman he'd known only one week.

AMY WAS DEEP in thought as she trudged down the stairs. Twenty-six years ago her father and mother must have been in this very shop, walking these streets that were fast becoming so familiar to her. She wondered what had drawn them to Marietta. True it was only a few hours from Yellowstone Park, where they'd met, but why pick this town in particular?

As she stepped out to the street, she paused to slip on her sunglasses.

"Amy!"

She turned at the sound of her name. Chet was just a few steps behind her. He looked calm and steady, his usual demeanor. But there was a glint of humor in his eyes.

"Shopping for a wedding dress?"

She glanced at the front window she'd admired earlier. "Right. I haven't found the groom yet, but I like being prepared."

He chuckled. "Did you stop in at the jewelry store to get your wedding bands while you were at it?"

"Actually I *was* at the jeweler's. I wanted to ask about this bracelet." She held out her arm to show him. "It was my mother's, and it was purchased right here in Marietta. I found the box it came in when I was sorting through my mother's things."

"Ah. Interesting. Your mother had a bracelet that was purchased in Marietta. I'm beginning to unravel the mystery of what brought you here. But there has to be more to the story than a bracelet."

Amy's instinct was to clam up. But then she realized how counterproductive that would be. The rodeo world was tight. Possibly Chet knew something about David Wilcox. He might even have met him.

"My mom raised me on her own. All I knew about my father was that Mom met him on a camping trip in Yellowstone. They were together for just a few weeks, and during that time he gave her this bracelet, which Mom wore every day. That was all I knew until after she died. I was cleaning out her room when I found the box the bracelet came in, along with a love letter signed simply with the letter 'D'."

Chet's eyes widened. "I get it now. You came to Montana to find your father."

That wasn't how she'd sold the move to herself. She needed a change, a chance to reinvent herself after the accident. But, she finally admitted, that was mostly window dressing. She *had* come to Montana to see if she could find her father.

"Yes."

"I hope you have more clues to his identity than a twenty-something-year-old bracelet and an initial?"

"I do. I have his name. It's a common name, though, and I had no way to focus my internet searches until I saw the Copper Mountain Rodeo program."

Chet looked surprised. "Hisis name was there?"

"Yes." She raised her sunglasses, so she could meet his gaze directly. "David Wilcox. Have you heard of him?"

Chapter Six

"Yeah, I've heard of David Wilcox," Chet said. "He's a rodeo legend. Is he really your father?"

"It's just my educated guess. I won't know for sure until I talk to him and find out if he had a fling with Helen Arden twenty-six years ago."

"Your mother never told him about you?"

"She tried. Sort of. Shortly after she found out she was pregnant, she sent him a letter. When she didn't hear from him, she didn't pursue it. They were both so young and they lived on opposite sides of the country. She decided to keep the baby—me—and raise me on her own."

It hadn't been easy for her mom. Her decision had caused a lot of friction with her parents—academics who lived in a large apartment on the Upper West Side. But eventually they got on board with the idea, allowing her mom to live with them while she completed her education. They'd even hired a nanny so her mother could pursue her PhD.

Amy had loved her grandparents, but in some ways they had reminded her of Emily and Richard from the *Gilmore*

Girls. They weren't as rich, but they were snobs and rather stuffy. It was a relief when her mom got tenure at NYU, and they could finally afford to move out to their own small apartment. Money was tight, but her mother had given her a home filled with love, security and lots of laughter. Amy knew she owed her mother everything. She'd tried to be a good daughter in return, and their bond had been tight.

But she did wonder why her mother had never married. She'd dated, yes, especially after Amy turned eighteen. But none of the men lasted more than a few months. "I get bored easily," her mother would say. Amy had always suspected there was more to it than that.

"I need to get back to Bramble House." She'd already taken more time off than she could afford.

"I'm headed there too."

As they walked, Amy tried not to feel self-conscious about her limp. It was subtle, but it did slow her down. She was glad Chet didn't say anything, just adjusted his pace to match hers.

"So David Wilcox," Chet began. "He was a legendary saddle-bronc rider back in his day. As a kid I was lucky enough to see him ride many times. He won at the national level at least twice, maybe more. About ten years ago he retired, and now he's a full-time rancher on a big spread just outside of Gardiner. I believe he's married and has a bunch of sons."

"Three sons," Amy supplied. When Chet raised his eyebrows, she elaborated, "That's what it says in this year's Copper Mountain Rodeo program." She paused, hit with a wallop of emotions she couldn't begin to untangle. "I could have brothers. Half brothers."

As a kid she'd longed for siblings. Now to find out about this other side of her family... Was she sad, excited, curious, nervous? All of the above and so much more.

"Hell of a thing if it turns out to be true," Chet said.

Yes, a hell of a thing, especially for someone like her, with no family left other than distant great-uncles and aunts and cousins she'd only met at her grandparents' funerals.

Once they reached Bramble House, they both paused at the point where the walkways to the main house and garage divided.

Though her chores awaited, Amy had one more important question to ask. "What kind of man is David Wilcox?"

"Top drawer. He has a solid reputation, not just as a cattleman and a former rodeo champion, but he also started the Big Sky Rodeo Academy where kids go to learn horsemanship and basic rodeo skills. Every year D. W. and his wife sponsor fifteen spots in their program for underprivileged kids."

"That's good to hear." But it was also intimidating. Suddenly this man who had only been a name to her when she was growing up was becoming a fully realized human being.

"Have you thought about how to approach him?"

"Not yet." The very idea panicked her. Didn't she have enough on her plate right now with the B & B?

"But you are going to contact him?"

"Yes. Maybe. I don't know. But right now I've got to get busy putting out my afternoon tea and coffee. And baking cookies," she added with determination.

"I see you made a dent in the lawn this morning," Chet said, glancing at the spot where she'd abandoned the mower. "I'll finish the job for you."

"You will not," she said, adopting her most imperious tone. "You are a guest, even if you are a reluctant one."

"Aw, Amy. I have nothing to do until it's time to go feed my horses again. I'd rather be busy than sitting in my room, bored."

"Can you imagine the way people in this town will gossip if they find out I'm putting my guests to work? No, Chet. I'll finish the lawn later."

AMY THOUGHT SHE'D been very clear. But fifteen minutes later, as she was creaming together a pound of butter with a mixture of brown and white sugar, she heard the mower start up.

She ought to be annoyed, but she couldn't help smiling.

It *would* be nice to have that job off her list today. So what if the locals talked? Probably nothing she did would meet with their approval anyway.

Twenty minutes later the mower turned off at just the moment she was pulling another failed attempt at cookies from her oven.

Darn it! She knew she'd followed every step of the simple recipe down to the letter. It was the same recipe she'd used as a kid and those cookies had always turned out perfectly. As she stared at the flattened blobs, she heard a knock at the kitchen's screen door. She turned to see Chet's face—minus his ubiquitous hat—on the other side of the screen.

"Butchered another batch have you?" He had the nerve to look amused.

Which only made her madder.

She threw up her hands in frustration. "I guess I better set up a full-time account at the Gingerbread and Dessert Shop on Main Street."

"Don't be too hasty." He opened the door and came inside. "My grandmother used to bake me a lot of chocolate chip cookies. She knew they were my favorite."

"That's sweet, Chet. But how is that relevant?"

"My grandmother lived just outside of Denver. Elevation in Denver is a bit over five thousand feet. Here in Marietta it's over four thousand feet. Whereas New York City, of course, is at sea level."

"And now we're talking geography. Fascinating stuff, Hardwick." Amy began scraping the ruined cookies into her composting bin. She hated thinking of all the butter, sugar, eggs and flour—not to mention chocolate chips—she'd wasted since moving to Bramble House.

"Here's the thing about living at high altitude." Chet did not seem at all fazed by her ill temper. "Air pressure is lower, which means liquids evaporate faster. Also, your leavening agent—in the case of cookies that'll be baking soda—is gonna expand more. If you don't add extra flour they'll end up collapsing."

Now she saw the relevance. "Into puddles. Like those." She pointed her spatula at the mess in the compost bin.

"Exactly."

"So what you're telling me is I have to add extra flour. But how much?"

He went to the sink to wash his hands. "Grandma's rule of thumb was two extra tablespoons per cup of flour. Come on, let's try it."

Was he serious? Amy consulted her watch. She had one suite to clean from top to bottom before the four o'clock check-in and it was already two thirty. "I don't have time. Besides, I have no more softened butter."

"This'll be fast, I promise." He'd already rolled up his sleeves and was washing the pile of dirty baking dishes she'd left in the sink. "My grandma always melted her butter in the microwave before adding the sugars."

"Seriously?" This did not sound right to her and she wasn't keen to waste another hour and another batch of ingredients.

"I'm not asking you to trust me, Amy. Just my grandmother. Now put a cup of butter in the microwave at low power, then get me two eggs please."

Amy stared at him. Was a real-life, handsome cowboy really standing in her kitchen purporting to teach her how to make chocolate chip cookies? She had to be dreaming. And since this wasn't real, she might as well do what he asked.

She put the butter in a large glass bowl and popped it into the microwave, then pulled out the eggs.

Chet finished drying all the measuring cups and bowls, then he asked her to turn the oven back on and line her baking sheets with parchment. By the time she'd done both those things he'd already added the eggs, the sugars and vanilla to the melted butter.

"Now we'll sift together the flour, salt and baking soda. But rather than sift, I just use a whisk."

"Do you have an Instagram account? Baking Tips From A Cowboy?"

"I don't do Instagram smart-ass. Now watch as I measure out the flour."

She watched. He added the required amount plus four tablespoons extra. And just five minutes later they had a new batch of cookie dough.

"You keep looking at your watch," Chet commented. "Am I keeping you from something?"

"I appreciate your help," she said, still not one hundred percent committed to the idea that this was reality, "but I've got to prepare a room for a guest checking in at four o'clock."

"Okay. You go ahead and clean. I'll stay here and bake. Nine minutes at three hundred and fifty degrees."

He was already dropping dollops of cookie dough onto the trays. Clearly this was out of her hands. Amy nodded, then went to gather her cleaning supplies. As she stripped the bed, her thoughts whirled. Discovering her father, the trip to the jeweler's, the singular relationship she seemed to be developing with her reluctant guest. Chet had taken her most remote room in order to avoid socializing, and yet he was turning out to be the friendliest person she'd met so far in Marietta.

Twenty minutes later she dashed back into the kitchen. The house was filled with the lovely scent of baking. And there was Chet, transferring perfectly shaped chocolate chip cookies onto the cooling racks.

A devilish light shone in his eyes as he took a cookie, broke it in half and offered one piece to her. "Quality control?"

The cookie was very warm, but not hot. She took a bite. And closed her eyes.

Yes. Yum. Oh, yes.

"These are good, Cowboy."

"Better than good. I see that look on a woman's face in two situations. One is when I bake her cookies. The other—"

He didn't finish. He didn't have to.

Anyway, now she knew. He was definitely flirting.

CHET WONDERED IF Amy knew she was blushing. She had an adorable blush. It really took the edge off her New York I-can-do-it-all attitude. But he knew her better now. Behind that attitude was a woman trying to find her footing after a tragic accident. If more people around here understood what she'd been through, they might be more sympathetic. But Amy had her pride. And he understood that.

What he didn't understand was what he was doing here, in her kitchen, baking her cookies and making her blush. If she survived her induction to Montana life, if she didn't go running back to the city within the year, she still wouldn't be the right woman for him. She was too well educated. Too citified. He doubted she would ever consider life with a lowly cowboy like him.

But logic seemed to take a back seat whenever he was around her.

"It's time for me to put out coffee, tea and cookies in the sitting room." She bustled around the kitchen, gathering the things she needed, then taking them out on a big tray. He washed the baking dishes for the second time, not minding a bit. He still had half an hour to kill before it was time to go see his horses.

He heard guests coming down the stairs, no doubt lured

by the scent of fresh baking. The front door opened, and more people spilled in. Amid the murmur of conversation Chet could hear Amy's voice as she chitchatted with the folks. She sounded cheerful. This must be a part of her job she actually enjoyed.

Chet dried the last of the measuring cups, then decided it was time to go. He was pulling open the screen door when Amy came back to the kitchen. Her tray was now empty except for two mugs of coffee and a couple of cookies.

"Wait. I want to thank you for teaching me about baking at elevation. And I saved you some cookies and a cup of coffee, if you have time." She set the tray on the counter.

He wasn't sure what looked more tempting. The hot coffee and fresh cookies. Or Amy smiling, looking relaxed and happy.

Actually he did know. It was Amy, hands down.

He took a seat at the counter and reached for the coffee. A hit of caffeine would go down well. "Folks out there sound like they're having a good time."

"They are. It's an interesting group. We've got a retired couple from Alberta, a film crew working on a documentary about small-town rodeos, and another couple whose daughter is a barrel racer. Best of all, they're all planning to stay for the rodeo so I won't have to turn over any more rooms until Sunday."

"Yeah?" He took a drink of coffee, then asked, "Does that free up some time for a riding lesson?"

She dropped her gaze. "Maybe. I don't know…"

"Horses are big animals. It's natural to be nervous if you haven't been around them. But I have a feeling you're going to love riding, Amy. And hey, if you really are the daughter of David Wilcox, this is a skill you need to learn."

She fixed her blue eyes on him. "I need to think about this."

"Maybe. Or you could come to the Circle C ranch with me right now. I spoke to Court this morning and he said they have just the horse for a beginning rider. He and Callan bought it for their five-year-old daughter Amelia. The horse is called Moonstruck."

"That's the name of one of my favorite movies."

"I'd take that as a sign."

Amy was visibly torn. She glanced back at the room where her guests were all gathered. Then at him.

"I'm trying hard to think of an excuse. But since you've mowed the lawn and baked the cookies, I guess I have no choice. Let's do it."

Chapter Seven

AMY HAD FALLEN in love with the mountains of Montana at first sight. They were rugged and craggy, imposing and spectacular. None more so than the peaks on either side of Paradise Valley. The Absarokas and the Gallatins. As Chet drove her south following the path of the mighty Yellowstone River, she was stunned by the beauty of it all.

"The Yellowstone is the longest undammed river in our country," Chet told her. "And this land, nestled between the two mountain ranges, is some of the best ranching land anywhere. Certainly the most beautiful."

Amy was dazed by the vastness of it all. Nowhere in the state of New York did the sky ever look so expansive, so blue, so fresh. This was called ranching country, and the homes were so far apart. For long stretches of time they saw nothing but undulating fields of wild grass stretching out to the forests growing on the flanks of the mountains. And then they'd pass a herd of cattle or horses. Several times they spotted mule deer, grazing right among the cattle.

"Do any of the ranchers grow crops like legumes and

grains rather than raise cattle?" Amy asked.

"Most of this land is non-arable," Chet explained. "Meaning even if the ranches weren't here, the land couldn't be used to grow food. Without cattle, you'd see more ungulates like elk and deer and moose. And bison."

"We pretty much wiped those out, didn't we?"

"They're making a comeback. But the populations will never be what they were—in the millions I've heard."

"Must have been something to see. Terrifying. But magnificent."

"Right?" He shot her a smile.

Amy wasn't ready for the drive to end when Chet started to slow his truck.

"Here already?"

"You sound disappointed."

"I wish we could keep driving all the way to Yellowstone," she admitted. She thought about her mother, making this trip all those years ago. No wonder she'd always spoken of Montana so fondly.

"I know that feeling," Chet said. "Wanderlust. Montana always does it to me, too."

As they drove through the Circle C ranch gate, she was impressed by the beauty of the two-story log home nestled amid some impressive tall pine trees. Chet drove past the house to a parking area near a grouping of freshly painted outbuildings.

Two horses came running up to the fence to meet Chet

when he got out of the truck. Amy stayed where she was, watching, impressed by the beauty of the horses and the obvious connection between them and Chet. But also intimidated by their size and their energy.

Chet waved at her to join them. Every instinct she possessed told her to stay put. But she fought the fear and forced herself to leave the safety of the truck. Tentatively she moved closer to the fence.

Chet was petting the horses like they were friendly Labrador retrievers. But these weren't dogs. They were huge animals. They tossed their heads and snorted, a message—she was certain—telling her to keep her distance.

"Bourbon is the sorrel, Hunter the chestnut," Chet explained.

Amy nodded, trying to work out what he meant. Sorrel must be the one with the lighter reddish coat. That horse had a white mark on its forehead. The darker horse had no markings on the face but its front legs looked like they were wearing white socks.

"They're very…big."

Only then did Chet seem to realize how nervous she was. He looked like he was going to urge her forward, but then he appeared to change his mind.

"These guys are competitors. They have a lot of energy. Let's go track down the mare Court suggested for you."

"Okay," she said reluctantly, wishing she had driven here in her own vehicle so she could turn around and leave right this second. She trailed Chet as he headed toward an enormous-sized barn—why did everything in Montana have to be so huge? Just then the barn door slid open and out walked a petite woman leading a sedate-looking black horse.

"Hey, Chet," the woman said. "Saw you drive up and thought I'd saddle Moonstruck for you. She'll appreciate a little attention and exercise. Amelia's spending the day with her cousins in town."

"Thanks." Chet accepted the reins, patting the horse's neck before making introductions.

"Callan, this is Amy Arden from Bramble House. Amy, Callan is Sage's youngest sister. She and her husband Court run this place."

"Court only thinks he runs it. It's really me." Callan winked as she shook Amy's hand. "So you're the New Yorker. Ever been on a horse before?"

Callan's grip was strong, belying her small stature and delicate features. This woman was tough, Amy realized. Inside and out.

"First time," she admitted. "And thinking maybe this isn't such a good idea after all."

"Aw, Moonstruck is gentle as a kitten. I wouldn't trust her with my little girl if she wasn't. And if you're gonna live in Montana, you ought to learn to ride."

Chet grinned. "That's what I told her."

"There must be lots of people in Montana who don't ride horses," Amy protested.

"Yeah, but think of all they're missing. Come, get acquainted." Chet beckoned her closer.

"I'll leave you to it," Callan said, turning back to the barn. "Have fun."

As if, thought Amy. All she wanted was to survive the experience. With small steps she moved closer to Chet. At least this horse seemed much quieter than the others.

"So, approaching a horse," Chet said. "First you want to make sure the horse sees you. Talk to her nice and low and quiet. Then approach from the front, at an angle."

"Hi, Moonstruck," Amy said, feeling awkward. "I'm Amy. Is it okay if I pet you?"

The horse responded by turning her head, just as Chet had said she would. Amy moved closer.

"That's right," Chet said encouragingly. "Now plant your hands on her shoulder. Come up nice and close."

Amy hesitated. Then she took a deep breath and planted both her hands on Moonstruck's shoulder. Nothing bad happened. Moonstruck's hair was coarse, her body strong and warm. Amy stroked the horse's shoulder. "That's a good girl."

The horse made a whickering sound and turned her nose toward Amy.

"Good," Chet said. "You're making a connection."

Chet passed her a chunk of carrot. "Hold your hand flat and offer this to her."

"Really?" Moonstruck had very big teeth, but Amy decided to trust him and do as Chet said. She only flinched a bit when Moonstruck took the treat.

"Great, you're doing great. Now I'll lead her into the pen and you can get in the saddle."

Amy had to force herself to move forward. Never had she been more aware of her limp, and that reminded her of the accident, the terror and the pain, and the heart-wrenching losses that followed.

Petting and feeding the horse was one thing. Getting up on its back, another. Yes, Moonstruck seemed gentle. But she was still a huge animal.

"I don't think I can do this, Chet. I'm terrified, and the horse is going to sense that."

Chet waited for her to enter the pen, then shut the gate. Still holding Moonstruck's reins, he turned to Amy. "Moonstruck is a calm, steady horse, and I'm right here beside you. That said, I don't want you getting on this horse if you're terrified."

"Good." He was letting her off the hook and she ought to feel relieved, but oddly what she felt was deflated.

"First though let me tell you what an older, more experienced cowboy once told me. Feeling scared is your choice. But you can also choose to feel brave."

The words sank in slowly. And she saw the truth in them. The choice was hers. She'd faced it when she'd made the decision to get behind the wheel of a car again. And though it had been hard, she had done it. And each time she'd gone for a drive, she'd found it easier.

Then again, she'd been driving since she was eighteen. And she'd never been on the back of a horse.

Her gaze drifted to the pastures beyond the round pen, to the forested areas of the foothills. There was so much to explore and appreciate.

And suddenly her choice was clear.

"I want to try," she told Chet.

"Okay." He guided her through each step, calm and patient. And before she knew it, she was up on the horse, her boots in the stirrups, her legs molded to the curve of Moonstruck's belly.

Instinctively Amy straightened her back. Engaged her core. For a few minutes Chet led her and Moonstruck around the pen then he said, "Enough of this. You're ready to take the reins."

After some brief instructions, she was on her own, just her and Moonstruck. For fifteen minutes she was content walking the horse in circles, then she gave a wistful look toward the open fields.

"Oh, no," Chet said, guessing what she was about to ask. "I promised I would take things easy for your first lesson. But don't worry. It won't be long before you're ready to go on a real trail ride. You've got great instincts. The way you sit in the saddle and steer through your core and legs."

Hours later, after brushing down Moonstruck, cleaning the tack and then watching as Chet took care of his own horses, Amy thought this had probably been her best day in Montana.

And every good thing had happened because of Chet. Or maybe what had made everything so good was simply being with Chet. Amy felt he was opening up around her and she was doing the same with him. What was happening felt special to her.

Did it feel that way to him too?

She was about to thank him for the great day, when a message pinged on his phone. He took it out of his back pocket and frowned.

"What's up?"

He stared out at nothing. Swallowed hard and then took a deep breath. "It's my dad. He just pulled into Marietta. Wants to know if he can stay with me."

AMY KNEW SOMETHING was wrong as soon as Chet parked out front of Bramble House about an hour before sunset. Several people were gathered on the front porch and they looked worried. She recognized her guests, Dusty and Penny Murphy. But Carol Bingley was there too. And a man she didn't recognize.

"What's going on?" Chet wondered.

He'd been silent for most of the drive home. When Amy told him she didn't mind if his father stayed in the room over the garage with him, all he'd said was, "Fat chance."

He'd told her his dad had a drinking problem years ago, but Amy didn't know if that was still the case. And she didn't dare ask. Chet's expression was flat and uninviting. He was even more of a closed book than when they'd first met.

Amy jumped out of the truck as soon as Chet put it into park. As she hurried toward the porch, she saw that everyone was standing around Penny, who was seated in a cushioned chair with her right leg supported on a stool. Dusty spotted her first.

"Hey there, Miss Amy. My wife's had a little accident." He turned to the other man on the porch, a man who Amy could now see was wrapping a tensor bandage around Penny's ankle. "This is Dr. Gallagher."

Amy barely glanced at the doctor. She went to Penny's side and took her hand. "What happened? Are you okay?"

"Very much okay," Penny answered brightly. "But it does appear I've injured my ankle."

"You'd better stay off it for a few weeks," the doctor said. "When you get home you might want to go for X-rays. But I'm almost certain it's just a sprain."

Amy's head was spinning. "How did you fall?"

Penny and Dusty exchanged a glance. It was clear they didn't want to say. But Carol Bingley had no such compunction.

"She tripped over a fold in the hallway rug. It's much too

dark in there. You really should replace that burnt-out light bulb."

"Oh no. I'm so sorry." Why, oh, why hadn't she let Chet replace the light bulb when he'd offered? She glanced behind herself to see if he had heard, but he was still at his truck, watching the proceedings but obviously keeping his distance.

Amy thanked the doctor for helping her guest.

"No problem. I was on my way home after my shift when the accident happened. Carol recognized my vehicle and waved me over." He turned back to Penny. "Not much more I can do for you now. Keep your foot elevated. Over-the-counter meds should be enough to keep the pain in control."

While Penny added her thanks to Amy's, Dusty drew Amy aside.

"I'm afraid we're going to have to abort our trip. I can't have Penny hobbling around the rodeo. She'll be more comfortable at home. Is there any way you could refund some of our money?"

"Of course! I'm so sorry about that burnt-out light bulb."

"Don't you fret about that. Accidents happen. I'm going to leave Penny here to rest and go pack our bags. We'll be on our way shortly. We have a good friend in Helena, who happens to be a nurse. She's offered us a bed for the night. Then by tomorrow evening we should be back in our own home."

Once Dusty left, Amy turned to Penny. "Can I get you something? Some water? A cup of tea?"

"I'm fine, dear. I'll just lounge here until my husband has the car packed." Penny sank back into the cushions. "After all this excitement, I'm suddenly exhausted. I'm afraid I'm going to sleep all the way to Helena."

"Let me know if you change your mind. I'd be happy to pack some snacks for your drive."

"We're so full after our dinner at the Graff. Don't you worry about us."

Amy rose, feeling dreadfully guilty. This time when she looked for Chet there was no sign of him. Not only that, his truck was gone too.

Unfortunately Carol Bingley hadn't gone anywhere. She took Amy by the arm and led her to the far end of the porch.

"It seems you're over your head, young lady. With these old houses it's important to stay on top of the regular maintenance and repairs. Never mind your yard. It took forever for you to finally mow your lawn and I don't suppose you'll ever get to the shrubs and flower beds. You really should hire some help."

Amy's mouth opened, but nothing came out. She was flabbergasted. First by this woman's absolute gall. And then by the suggestion she hire help. Hadn't Carol heard about the mass exodus? Perhaps the town gossip mill wasn't as efficient as she'd thought.

"I would love to have help," she finally managed. "But

the entire staff quit on my first day."

Carol blinked. "Really? That's not the story going around town."

"Oh?"

"I heard you let them go." Carol frowned. "Or maybe it *was* the other way, come to think of it."

Suddenly Amy felt as exhausted as Penny looked. She'd had enough of small-town gossip for the day. "Carol, thank you for helping my guests. But you'll have to excuse me. I've got work to do."

And first on the list was changing that darn light bulb.

Chapter Eight

Every small town had a bar like the Wolf Den and Chet had been in a lot of them during his life thanks to his old man. As he pulled open the door, he was hit with the vile smell of stale alcohol, old frying oil, and grilled burgers. The combination reminded him of too many nights he'd gone looking for his father, wondering if there was money for his supper and was he supposed to sleep in the truck or what?

Thankfully he hadn't had to depend on his father for food for too many years. He'd started picking up odd jobs when he was ten and by sixteen he'd been fully independent. But walking into a place like this brought back some of the worst of his memories.

He stopped to let his eyes adjust to the dim lighting, and his ears to the loud outlaw country music playing on the sound system.

First he focused on the bar, studying the patrons, and dismissing them. Then he examined the people sitting at tables and the perimeter booths.

He wasn't there.

Chet checked his phone again.

I'll wait for you at the Wolf Den. You can buy me dinner.

Once more, Chet scanned the room, this time quickly, convinced his father had stood him up. Wouldn't be the first time.

A small, old man at the bar gave him a wave. Chet did a double take.

Damn it, that *was* the old man. Reluctantly he stepped forward. They didn't hug or even shake hands. That would have been much too civilized for Walt Hardwick.

Walt patted the stool next to his. "Sit."

Like a dog, Chet obeyed. But he couldn't take his eyes off his father. It had been around five years since he'd seen him last and during that time his father had lost a ton of weight. He seemed shorter, too, though he'd never been a tall man. He had the skin of a man ten years older than his sixty-five years. And it had an unhealthy yellow cast.

"Want a beer?" his father asked.

Chet shook his head.

"Well I'll have one if you're paying. A burger and fries as well."

Chet caught the bartender's attention and placed the order for his father.

"And for yourself?" the barkeep asked.

"Nothing." He couldn't eat here. He'd get sick. He waited for his father to tell him what he wanted. Besides the free meal.

"So what you got to say for yourself?" his father asked.

"Not much. What's new with you?"

"Nothing new. Same shit as ever."

The beer arrived and Walt wasted no time putting it down and asking for another.

"So what are you doing here?" Chet finally asked.

"Can't a man come visit his son? I saw you were competing and I drove up to watch."

"Drove up from where?"

"Does it matter?"

Chet thought about that. Decided it didn't.

When the burger arrived, Walt took just a few bites before pushing it aside. "Seems like you're not competing as much as you used to."

Chet was surprised he'd paid enough attention to notice. "I'm getting old. Thinking of giving it up soon."

"You call thirty old?" Spittle flew from the older man's mouth. "Wait 'til you're my age."

"Rodeo's a young man's sport. I don't want to end up all crippled and arthritic."

"Yeah, well they tell me you got yourself a college degree. Been giving advice to all the cowboys on how to save for retirement and shit like that."

Chet felt his jaw clench tight. He took a deep breath. "What of it?"

"Nothing. Just repeating what I heard." He downed a

french fry, finished his second beer. "You like your chances for the tie-down? I see Pete Proctor's on the schedule. He'll be tough to beat."

Chet wondered how much more of this he would have to take before his father finally asked for whatever it was he wanted. But the minutes dragged on, and Walt asked for another beer and still no request was forthcoming.

By eight Chet couldn't take it anymore. "I got to get going. I'm up early to look after my horses."

"Where you sleeping?"

Chet did not want to say. "Why?"

"Been bunking out in my truck the last few nights. Be good to sleep in a bed for a change. Maybe take a shower."

So he'd been serious. The old man really did want to stay with him. Chet wanted to say no. He really did. Being around the old man was toxic for him. And he really didn't want him anywhere near Amy.

But, low-down skunk that he was, this was his father.

"There's a pull-out couch in my room."

"Great, you can have that. I'll take the bed."

IT WAS ALMOST dark, but Chet could see Amy sitting on her front porch as he pulled up his truck to the bed-and-breakfast. His father parked his old beater right behind him and Chet felt his gut tighten as he imagined what Amy must be thinking.

He got out of his truck slowly and ignoring his father who was pulling a backpack from his truck, he went to see Amy. He noticed she had a glass of wine tonight with just a splash left in it.

"How are you doing? Was your guest okay?"

"I wasn't sure you cared. After you took off like that." Amy finished the wine and set the glass down on a table. "My guest had a sprained ankle. She tripped in the hallway, the hallway that was too dark because I hadn't yet changed the light bulb."

"Damn, I'm sorry." He should have changed that for her, even though she'd told him not to.

"No." She put up her hand. "It's not your fault. Don't you dare apologize. Anyway, the guests have left—they're driving back to Canada." Her gaze shifted to something—or someone—behind him. "Is that your…"

It cost Chet all his nerve to turn and acknowledge his father. The old man was moving slowly, looking like most every bone in his body was hurting. His father was the perfect example of what hard living and too much rodeo could do to a man.

"Amy, this is my father Walt. I was wondering if he could bunk in my room with me for the night."

"Oh." Amy stood and took a long look at the man behind him before saying, "Hello, Mr. Hardwick."

"Good evenin', ma'am."

She turned back to Chet. "Of course your father can stay with you. Would you like an extra key?"

"That won't be necessary," Chet said. "Though it looks like I'll be needing that extra towel after all."

WHILE HIS FATHER was in the shower, Chet went outside to see if Amy was still on the porch. She was. And she'd refilled her wineglass.

"I'm sorry to bring a man like my father to your bed-and-breakfast," he began. "Tomorrow I'll try and find him a motel room."

"You don't have to do that."

He went a few steps closer. Paused on the bottom rung of the porch stairs. Amy had showered and changed since this afternoon. Even from here he could smell her clean scent, layered with her sweet exotic perfume. He felt a deep longing and a sadness. Maybe in an alternate universe, one where his mother didn't die and his father didn't drink, he and Amy would have had a chance.

"He's a drunk and a liar and a freeloader. Believe me, you don't want him here." *And neither do I.*

"He's a lot older than I expected."

"He's sixty-five."

"I would have guessed eighty. Is he sick?"

"Nah, just too much booze and tobacco and every other

bad habit you can think of." He was tired. Ready to go to bed. But he didn't want to go back to his room until the old man was flaked out.

As if she sensed his reluctance to leave Amy offered him a glass of wine. Then remembering he didn't drink she added, "I could make you some coffee."

Shame that she had seen his father, the man with whom he shared fifty percent of his DNA, kept him where he was. "That's fine. I should leave you in peace." He was turning to leave, intending to take a late-night stroll along the river, but her voice called him back.

"I never had a chance to thank you for today. For the riding lesson. I was terrified at the beginning."

He grinned. "I noticed."

"You must think I'm a real scaredy-cat but I didn't used to be this way. In fact, I was almost too fearless. Or so my mother said." Her bottom lip trembled. She took another sip of wine.

He guessed it was the accident that had changed her, and he understood. He'd seen the same thing happen to many of his rodeo colleagues. After a bad fall some of them shook it off and went back in the ring as soon as they could. For others it was harder. And took longer. Or didn't happen at all.

"That's okay," he said. "You might have been scared. But you rose above it. You got on the horse. And you did great."

"Thanks. You're being kind. I bet nothing ever scares

you."

"Not true. I've been scared silly lots of times. So far, I've been lucky—all my injuries have been minor. But each passing year and each new rodeo is beginning to feel like a spin of the roulette wheel."

"So why don't you stop spinning?"

"Yeah. I've been asking myself that." Then, because he didn't want to talk about himself or his future prospects—which looked bleak to him right now—he asked if she was going to keep up the riding lessons.

"I'd like to. Any chance I could get another lesson tomorrow?"

She had caught the bug. And he'd have loved to give her a lesson tomorrow and every other day she wanted, but reality had come knocking today and it had broken down the door. "I may have my hands full with my father. But I'm sure you could find another teacher. I'll ask Sage who she recommends."

Amy looked at him in silence. He could see her swallow. Take a deep breath.

"It's getting late. I better go prep my breakfast."

He nodded. Took a backward step.

"Oh wait. I almost forgot." She tossed something at him. "Here's your extra towel."

"Thanks." He waited for her to go inside before heading back to his room. The lights were all off. It should be safe to go inside.

He knew his father had an ulterior motive for tracking him down to Marietta. It was probably money. Chet wondered how much he'd want this time. He wished he could tell the old man to go to hell. He'd worked hard to save his money and it was supposed to be the starter fund for the next stage in his life. Whatever that was going to be.

But he'd probably do what he'd done all the other times, just to get rid of him and the toxic effect of his presence on Chet's life. He'd grit his teeth. And fork over the cash.

Chapter Nine

IN BED THAT evening, with the windows wide open and the overhead fan going at full speed, Amy read the first few chapters of the Bramble family history book that Eliza had written. It was more interesting than she expected. She had to admire the courage of Henry and May Bell Bramble who had left their civilized life in Boston to build a new home and life in the wilds of Montana. Though she was captivated by the chapter about the twins who died under suspicious circumstances in 1950, Amy's burning eyes forced her to set the book aside.

The next morning Amy went about her usual routine, but when she tried to drop off Chet's coffee and muffins no one answered her knock. She looked for his truck and saw that it was gone, as well as his father's.

Chet had made it pretty clear what he thought of his father. He'd said he had a rough childhood and Amy was willing to bet it had been even worse than he'd admitted. Most men would have cut all ties with a father like that. It said a lot about Chet that he hadn't.

The man was noble to a fault. But also kind and soft-hearted. You could see it in his eyes.

She headed back to the kitchen, despondent. Yesterday she'd felt such a wonderful connection building between her and Chet. But from the moment he'd heard from his father, Chet had grown cool and distant.

Maybe things would improve again once Walt Hartwick left town. But Chet was only in Marietta for five days. After the rodeo he'd be gone. And she'd probably never see him again.

Amy went inside to serve breakfast to her other guests. This morning everyone came down at the same time, which was helpful. As usual Graham and Rick sat down and immediately got on their phones. Lucy, however, was excited about a wedding they were going to film later that morning.

"Who's getting married?" Amy asked.

"Remember the couple who came by Bramble House yesterday morning?"

"Jake Richards and Willow McBride?" Her face warmed as she remembered how she'd ushered them out of her house and then shut the door in their faces.

"Yes. That's them. They're getting married today, then competing in the rodeo on the weekend. Isn't that crazy romantic?"

"Did you say Willow McBride?" Fred asked. "She's going to be facing off with our daughter in the barrel racing. Supposed to be one tough competitor."

"Who's your daughter?" Lucy asked.

"Ruby Lancaster. She's relatively new to the circuit. This is just her second year."

"Oh, we must interview her too. What do you think, Graham?"

"For sure." Graham stopped scrolling on his phone to focus on Fred and Sue. "Can you set something up?"

"We can take you to meet her right after breakfast," Fred offered. "She's staying out of town at Wilder Dreams."

"Is that Tucker Wilder's ranch?" Lucy asked.

"Sure is. Lucy's going to be doing some practice runs with Tucker," Sue explained.

"Oh wonderful! We already have an interview set up with Tucker for later in the day. We'll interview Ruby at the same time." Lucy rubbed her hands together. "Synchronicity at work. I love it."

"Ruby will be so pleased to be included." Sue glanced around the table, then turned to Amy. "What happened to that couple from Alberta? Dusty and Penny Murphy? We had plans to meet up this morning and take a tour through the scenic Paradise Valley."

Fred craned his neck to look out the window. "Their car is gone."

Amy twisted the cloth in her hands. "I'm afraid Penny tripped in the hallway yesterday and sprained her ankle."

"Probably because she couldn't see well. I've been meaning to tell you that light bulb was burned out," Fred said.

"Yes, well, I've replaced it, but unfortunately not soon

enough. The Murphys left last night, wanting to get back to Canada in case Penny needed medical attention. Thankfully though it sounds like that won't be necessary. Dusty texted me this morning to say Penny was doing much better."

"Oh, I'm glad," Sue said. "But I'm sorry they had to cut their trip short. We had planned to attend the rodeo together."

Amy was sorry too. She'd also enjoyed the older couple's company and was sad their trip had been aborted.

Also, now she had a vacant room she needed to fill.

After breakfast she cleaned the Murphys' room, started laundry and then went outside to try and figure out what Carol Bingley thought she should be doing with the shrubs and the perennials.

On close inspection she had to agree the shrubs were overgrown and the beds were full of weeds. But she knew so little about gardening, she had no idea where to start. So instead, she went to the porch, to water the potted flowers. She'd just finished when she noticed a tall, slim woman with a thick braid of red hair walking her way.

When their eyes met the other woman waved. Amy put down the hose and waited.

"Hi, I'm Sage Carrigan. You must be Amy?"

"I am." She smiled, but she couldn't help feeling wary. No doubt Carol Bingley had already spread the story about Penny Murphy's accident through town. One more strike against the incompetent new B & B owner.

"Do you have a few minutes?" Sage asked.

"Sure. Come sit down. Would you like something to drink?"

"I'm fine, thanks." Sage took a good look around the porch before sliding a small backpack off her shoulders and settling into a chair. "It's so strange not to see my great-aunt Mable out here. She loved sitting out on the porch on beautiful summer mornings."

Amy perched on a chair at a ninety-degree angle from Sage. "How long has your aunt been gone?"

"It's been over four years. She could be imperious, sometimes demanding, but she was the last of her generation and we all miss her."

"I've seen pictures of her. She reminds me a bit of the dowager on *Downton Abbey*."

Sage laughed. "In looks *and* personality, I assure you. My sisters and I thought she should have tried out for the part and given Maggie Smith a run for her money."

Amy laughed too. It was impossible not to like Sage. But she'd better not relax too much until she found out the purpose behind Sage's visit.

"I'm sorry I missed you when you came by the shop the other day. I've been meaning to come round and introduce myself. Now that you've bought Bramble House, you're practically one of the family."

Amy was stunned. Pleasantly so. This was the friendliest any of the Carrigan-Brambles had been since she arrived.

"Thank you," she finally managed. "I hope to take good care of the place. But it's been a bumpy start to be honest."

"You're referring to the staff walking out on you?"

"That would be the main thing," she agreed. "Though to be fair, my inexperience hasn't helped. My MBA hasn't been very useful when it comes to high-altitude baking and changing light bulbs. Among other things."

"You poor thing. You were really thrown into the deep end weren't you?"

Sage was so sympathetic, but Amy was cautious about letting her guard down. "Is there anything in particular you want to talk to me about?"

"Not really. To be honest, it was Chet who pointed out you'd had a less than friendly welcome to our town. I may be a little late, but I'm trying to rectify that. Oh, I almost forgot." She opened the backpack she'd been carrying with her and pulled out a small copper-colored box. "I bought you a little treat. For you, mind you. Not the guests."

"Thank you." Amy tucked the box into the shade.

"Pop them into the fridge later," Sage said, "to preserve their quality. Anyway, after my talk with Chet I gave Ella a call. When I asked her why she and the others had quit, she said they were annoyed by all the changes you wanted to make."

"Really? Because I'm not proposing much. Some new art, more imaginative names for the bedrooms and a fresh coat of paint. I'm even planning on using heritage colors."

"That doesn't exactly sound drastic," Sage agreed. "It's funny, I think the staff are more protective of the B & B than my family is. But maybe if you had tried *consulting* them about the changes."

"Yes." Amy knew this from her experience in business. A new owner should not come into a situation with an imperial top-down approach. Not if she wanted buy-in from the existing employees. "I was just so excited about the possibilities."

"I get that," Sage said. "By the way, my sister Callan mentioned Chet brought you out to the Circle C yesterday for a riding lesson."

"Yes. I was petrified to be honest. But Chet's an amazing teacher."

"I bet he is. Too bad he is only planning to stay in town until Sunday. Then again, maybe he'll enjoy Marietta so much he'll make it his permanent home when he retires from the rodeo. Like Dawson and I did."

Was this aimed at her? Amy wondered. A gentle hint that she might have a future with Chet if she wanted?

"Chet did seem to be enjoying Marietta," she replied cautiously. "Until his father showed up last night. Now I suspect he can't wait to hit the road and be done with the place."

Sage's nose wrinkled. "Walt Hardwick's in Marietta? That man is a disgrace. A real ball and chain around Chet's ankle."

"Chet mentioned his mother died when he was born."

"Yes. So sad. He lived with his maternal grandmother until he was around eight. But then she passed, and his father got full custody."

"Chet hasn't said a lot but I gather Walt was a negligent dad."

Sage hesitated. "Chet's a private man, but it sounds like he's already opened up to you some. I can't tell you how rare that is."

"We're very different people. But I find him surprisingly easy to talk to."

"I'm glad. Chet is a wonderful man. And yes, his father was negligent. Beyond negligent, actually. Walt was also cruel and sometimes abusive. Chet was already eighteen when I met him and well rid of his father, but some of the rodeo old-timers have told me stories about Chet spending nights sleeping in the truck while Walt tied one on in the scuzzy bars he liked to frequent. Summer and *winter*," she added.

"That's horrible." Amy imagined an eight-year-old boy shivering in a cold truck in freezing weather, waiting and waiting and waiting…

"And there were beatings," Sage added. "Over the years various people reported Walt to the authorities, but he'd promise to do better and then he'd move to a new district and somehow he kept eluding the law."

"Poor Chet." Her heart felt crushed as she thought of the

young boy, grieving for his grandmother, getting thrown to the wolves in the guise of his father.

"Yes. The system failed Chet, that's for sure."

"Why do you think his father didn't give him up to the authorities? It doesn't sound like he enjoyed the responsibility of having a child."

"Probably so he could get his hands on Chet's grandmother's estate," Sage speculated. "But I feel weird talking about Chet's private affairs like this."

"Sorry. I shouldn't have asked so many questions."

"It's okay. I can tell you care about him."

"I do," Amy admitted. "And I appreciate you trusting me enough to fill me in. It sure explains a lot. Though, after all you've told me about Walt, I'm surprised Chet let him share his room last night."

"Chet is such an honorable person. And Walt has mastered the art of exploiting that to his own benefit." Sage shook her head. "My husband's a deputy and he's seen firsthand what happens to kids who suffer abuse. Some are amazingly resilient while others turn into violent abusers themselves. And then there are the more sensitive ones, who end up feeling guilty and ashamed. As if the abuse was *their* fault."

It was pretty clear to Amy into which category Chet fell. "When I first met him I thought Chet seemed so strong, maybe even overconfident. I had no idea of the pain he was masking."

"Chet is strong. And disciplined, and smart. Dawson and I both think so highly of him. And he is confident about some things. Like his abilities as a tie-down roper and a wrangler and a financial planner."

"Financial planner?" That was a surprise.

"Yes, I gather the financial insecurity of his youth motivated him to take online college courses so he could learn all about economics, investing and taxes. A lot of guys on the circuit go to him for saving and investing advice, I've heard."

"That's impressive."

"Right? He's good at so many things. But underneath all that are the scars from his childhood. There are lots of us who love him. But he only lets us get so close and no further. It's like he draws a line."

Amy nodded. Chet had certainly drawn a line with her after his father showed up. Thanks to Sage, she now understood why. But that didn't make it hurt any less.

AMY WAS BAKING a double batch of chocolate chip cookies that afternoon when the reservation line rang. She wiped her hands clean and went to the front desk to answer the call.

"Bramble House, Amy speaking."

"Hey there," a man with a deep, gritty voice replied. "This is a long shot, but do you have a room available for the weekend? I'd like to check in tomorrow night so I can go to the parade Saturday morning."

"You must be heaven sent. I had a room free up yesterday." She wouldn't mention, of course, that the room was available because she had negligently not replaced a burnt-out light bulb. "It's got a queen bed if that's okay."

"That's great, even a single would do. My wife was going to come with me, but she's running late on her current project."

"The queen room is all I've got." Amy quoted the price. "Will that do?"

"Yup. Let me give you my credit card info." He read off the numbers, the expiration date and the security code from the back.

Amy copied everything down carefully. "And your name?"

"Oh yeah. Guess I forgot the most important part. David Wilcox from Gardiner, Montana."

"Did you say David Wilcox?"

"Sure did."

Amy's mouth went dry. She sank back into her chair. She was almost certain that she was on the phone with her biological father. It was unreal. But also nerve-racking. And exciting. She honestly didn't know whether she was happy or sad, only that her stomach felt gutted and her heart was pumping like she was on the final stretch of a marathon.

"So...are we good?" David Wilcox finally said, breaking the long silence.

"We're good." She answered mechanically, in a voice that didn't even sound like her own. "I'll see you tomorrow."

"Look forward to it."

After the call, Amy sat in that chair for a long time. More than anything she wanted to talk to her mom. She regretted now not asking more questions about her father when she'd had the chance. He'd seemed such a shadowy figure when she was growing up. More like a fictional character than a real person.

But David Wilcox was indeed real.

And tomorrow she was going to meet him.

AMY DIDN'T SEE Chet until sunset that evening. She was on the porch as usual, eating one of the chocolates Sage had given her—a creamy milk chocolate and caramel confection with a dash of sea salt on top.

Despite another beautiful sunset and the delicious treat, she was having a hard time finding a sense of peace this evening. She wasn't sure which was causing her more stress: the upcoming visit from the man she thought was her father, or the new tension between her and Chet.

As she watched him drive up and park in his usual spot, she looked to see if his father was with him. But Chet was alone. As he got out of his truck, he glanced her way. She waved, hoping he would come join her. Or at least wave back.

For the longest time he stood by the truck. With his hat and strong profile silhouetted against the night sky he looked like he belonged in a poster of the old west. Why had she never found cowboys appealing before? Or maybe it was just him. There was something so solid and yet lonely about him. It pulled at her heart.

Finally, he crossed the street and came halfway up the path.

"That sunset never gets old, does it?" he said.

"Another gorgeous evening."

He slipped a thumb through the belt loop of his jeans. His features were strained, telegraphing tension. Rather than asking if he wanted to join her, Amy left her chair and went down the stairs, holding the railing to compensate for her bum leg.

"Have you heard from the Murphys?" he asked.

"Dusty just sent me a text. They arrived home in time for dinner. The swelling is already going down in Penny's ankle, thankfully."

"Good news. What about that vacant room? Any chance you can fill it before the weekend?"

"Funny you should ask. A crazy thing happened today. This guy called out of the blue for a reservation. And you know who it was?"

A small smile played on Chet's mouth. "This sounds like it's gonna be good. Is it someone famous?"

"Even better. It was David Wilcox."

"No!" Chet whistled. "Is that fate or what?"

"Right? I'm so nervous I don't know what to do. He's coming tomorrow. I can't decide whether to tell him about my mom right away or wait."

"What if he claims not to remember her?"

She'd thought of every possibility. "I won't press it. I don't have any way to prove I'm his daughter without a DNA test. But even if he agreed to that, what's the point of finding a father who doesn't want to be found?"

"Ha. I wish my father didn't want to be found."

After hearing the extra details from Sage, Amy didn't blame him. "So where is he?"

"Managed to find a room for him at the motel by the gas station. It'll be noisy, near the highway, but he'll probably have enough booze in him he won't notice." He spoke with so much bitterness, Amy's heart ached.

"Has he always had a problem with alcohol?"

"For as long as I can remember." Chet kicked a pebble off the walkway. Let out a dispirited sigh.

"What's he doing in Marietta anyway? Did he just come to see you?"

"That's what he claims. Wants to watch me compete. But he'll be hitting me up for cash at some point. And then he'll disappear, and I won't see him for a few more years. It's our usual pattern."

"Doesn't sound like much of a father." She hesitated. "I

was talking to Sage today. She told me a bit about what he was like when you were a kid. She wasn't gossiping. She could tell we were becoming friends and she wanted me to understand some of what you've been through."

"Sage and Dawson are good people. My father is not. It's as simple as that."

"And yet you are still good enough to help your father when he needs it."

"I don't do it out of niceness or kindness. It's obligation. It's a trap. He's my father and I can't change that."

There were some people, lots of people, Amy suspected, who wouldn't be so generous. On the other hand, maybe giving money to an alcoholic wasn't doing him any favors. "Do you worry you're just feeding his habit?"

"Maybe I am, but he always claims to need the money for something. Truck repairs, gambling debts, taxes. I have no way to know if he's telling the truth or lying. Maybe I just give him the money so he'll go away."

She put her hand on his arm, felt the tension in his muscles, the heat of his skin. "You give him the money because you're a kind man. A good son. Much better than your father deserves."

Chet met her gaze then and she felt his burning scrutiny. His gaze dipped to her lips and her heart went crazy.

"You're so damn pretty, Amy. And easy to talk to. I know I shouldn't be hanging around, wasting your precious fifteen minutes."

"What if I like having you hang around?" She wanted him to kiss her. Her hand was still on his arm and she could feel him leaning in closer. His gaze kept going to her eyes, her mouth, and back again.

"I'd say you could do better."

"Why don't you let me be the judge and kiss me?"

He groaned. "God help me, maybe I will."

They moved at the same time, closing the gap. Him bending down, her straining up, connecting in the middle. A gentle kiss at first, then just as she could feel herself on the verge of being subsumed, he suddenly let go. Stepped back.

"Sorry, Amy. I shouldn't have done that."

"I thought…we both did that." The air had gone suddenly cool. She glanced to the horizon. The sun had set. It would soon be dark.

He took another step back and her hand fell from his arm. It had been a wonderful kiss. Hadn't it? Why was he pulling back?

Then Sage's words came to her. *There are lots of us who love him. But he only lets us get so close and no further. It's like he draws a line.*

Chet was doing it again. Drawing a line. And it hurt. She had thought she was becoming something special to him. The way he was to her.

She watched as he retreated to his hideaway in the room above the garage. He didn't even glance back once before disappearing inside.

And suddenly she felt very, very lonely. She missed her mother. She missed her colleagues and her college girlfriends. This was such vast, wild country and she was totally on her own. Not even a staff member to chat with as she put together the spinach and cheese strata for the next morning, using one of Eliza's starred recipes.

Finally in her room, with all her chores complete, she pulled out the love letter to her mother. This, and the bracelet, were all she had from her father. And tomorrow she was going to meet him. What would he be like? Would they have an instant connection? What if she didn't like him...or he her?

Before going to sleep, Amy tucked the silver bracelet safely inside its box. She wouldn't wear it tomorrow. Just in case he recognized it. She wanted to be in control of events as much as possible.

Chapter Ten

AMY WAS UP early the next morning. She'd slept better than she'd expected. Pure exhaustion could do that. She wondered how long she could keep up this pace, doing everything by herself. The irony was, she was so busy, she didn't have time to hire new staff.

After a quick morning shower, she went downstairs to start the coffee and defrost muffins. The supply in the freezer would last one or two more days, but then she was going to need to bake more. She sure hoped it didn't take as long to master high-altitude muffins as it had cookies.

She had Chet's coffee and muffins ready a half hour earlier than normal and as she stepped outside, she caught him on his way to his truck.

"Here, you can take these with you." She handed him the thermos and bag of muffins.

He barely met her eyes. "Thanks, but you shouldn't bother. You're too busy as it is."

Dark stubble outlined his jaw, and circles under his eyes betrayed a poor night's sleep. Yet he still looked gorgeous to her.

"It's my job," she reminded him. "What Sage and Dawson paid me for."

He accepted this with a nod. "Well, thanks. Your coffee is a lot better than the stuff they brew at the gas station on the way out of town."

"Is that where you went yesterday?" She shook her head. "Bad mistake."

He almost relaxed. Almost smiled. Then his lips tightened, and his shoulders squared. "I better get going. Good luck with David Wilcox."

"Maybe you'll be back by the time he checks in? I could use some moral support."

She couldn't tell what he was thinking as he gazed at her. Then he lifted one shoulder. "Maybe."

And he left.

IT WAS DIFFICULT for Amy to focus the rest of the day. First, she burnt the bacon, which set off the smoke alarm, which brought several neighbors running, including Carol Bingley.

"My goodness, girl," Carol said, as she flapped a tea towel near the alarm to disperse the smoke. "You should cook your bacon in the oven. Three hundred and fifty degrees for thirty minutes. Never fails. Never burns."

Amy, who wasn't quite sure why Carol was in her kitchen—she knew she hadn't invited her—put her hand firmly on Carol's shoulder and guided her toward the screen door. "I'll try that. Thanks, Carol. And thanks for coming to help, but all is good now, so I'll let you get on with your day."

Before leaving, Carol said through the screen door, "Let me know when you have time to tackle your perennials. I'll be happy to show you how to divide them."

"Will do, thanks again." Amy had no idea what Carol meant by dividing perennials. She'd have to do an internet search when she had a minute.

Amy set out the strata and fruit salad and muffins on the buffet for people to help themselves. The Lancasters were the first people down. As she poured their coffee she said, "I'm sorry there's no bacon this morning. It came out a little…crisp."

"That explains the ruckus with the smoke alarm." Fred laughed. "Don't worry. You've got plenty of food without it."

Next down were Lucy and Graham. They chatted amicably with the Lancasters as they heaped their plates with food. They were all excited about the welcome dinner and street dancing that would be happening later that evening.

"Will you be going, Amy?" Lucy asked.

"If I have time." But she wouldn't try too hard to make it. She had no one to go with and sitting by herself watching others have fun would only make her feel lonelier than she already was.

It took forever to clean the cast-iron griddle she'd used

for the bacon. She thought she might give Carol's method a try the next morning. There was always a kernel of genuine helpfulness behind her interference. And it was nice to know that Bramble House would never burn down—not with Carol on guard.

As she washed dishes, Amy gazed out the window at the beautiful summer day. The weather was calling her. She wondered if she'd ever have the time to go for a hike or pursue her riding lessons. But the bathrooms needed cleaning and the kitchen floor scrubbing. This was not how she'd pictured spending her new life as a B & B owner. Not how Eliza had described her days in her binder.

With a cook and a cleaner and a gardener on staff, Eliza had focused on office work and interacting with her guests. These were the jobs Amy felt qualified for. The jobs she actually enjoyed.

Amy kept an eye on the time as she did the housework. Thanks to being distracted, she left the water running in the laundry tub, and it overflowed, creating a huge puddle that required mopping and towel drying. Then when she put the towels in for a wash, she accidentally added the bleach to the fabric softener holder. So the towels had to go for a second wash and came out with white blotches from the bleach.

At this rate she wouldn't have time to shower and change and put on a little makeup before David Wilcox arrived. She hoped he wouldn't be one of those guests who showed up hours before check-in time. What a crazy day.

Chet was worried about Hunter, the horse he'd planned to ride for his first go on Saturday. His horse seemed keyed up, stressed. He gave Sage a call. "I was wondering if you and Dawson could help me get some practice time in with my horse, Hunter? I hate to ask, and I'm sure you're busy…"

"It's no problem," Sage assured him. "Dawson isn't on duty, and we were already thinking about going for a trail ride. We can be at the Circle C within the hour."

Chet passed the time by giving his other horse, Bourbon, a nice, long trot. He was just saddling up Hunter when Sage and Dawson arrived.

"Hey, Chet," Sage said. "Sorry we're a bit late. Dawson's mother and her husband are spending the day in Bozeman, but they were slow hitting the road."

"Your horses look good," said Dawson. He was tall for a former rodeo cowboy. In his day he'd competed at both the tie-down and saddle-bronc riding. Chet still felt a bit of the awe he'd had for the man as a teenager.

"Horses are in good shape," Chet agreed. "Just hope the rider doesn't let them down."

"As if." Dawson clasped him on the shoulder. "You got this, buddy."

Chet wished he shared the other man's confidence. Normally one day out from a rodeo he was laser-focused on his horses and the job before them. This time was different.

His thoughts kept straying. One moment he was worrying about his old man and wondering how much he was going to hit him up for this time. The next he was daydreaming about Amy, wishing she could be here with him right now.

He'd love to be able to explain the fine art of tie-roping to her. Besides being accurate with a rope, you also needed to be a good horseman, a fast sprinter. The sport had developed out of the need for wranglers to single out sick or injured calves to give them veterinary treatment. The calf's well-being was always paramount.

Stop talking to Amy in your head, he ordered himself. She wasn't here. But Sage and Dawson were. And they were waiting for him to get himself and his horse into position. He maneuvered Hunter into the box next to the chute with the calf, then gave Dawson a nod.

The calf started running. Chet reined in Hunter, waiting for the calf to gain the appropriate head start before they broke through the barrier. As his horse charged ahead, Chet circled his rope, waiting for the right moment.

Now. He felt a thrill as the rope slid around the calf's neck. As soon as the loop tightened, Hunter braked. Chet dismounted and Hunter took a few backward steps, tightening the rope, but not too much. What a good boy. Chet flanked the calf then whipped the pigging string around three of the calf's legs. He jumped up throwing his arms in the air to show he was done. Then back to his horse to slacken the rope and make sure the calf was good and tied.

"Awesome!" Sage called out. "Seven point five, Chet."

"That's real good," Dawson agreed. "Want to have another go?"

The calf had already freed himself and was trotting out of the pen in search of his mother. Chet patted his horse on the neck. "Naw. If my horse gets it right the first time, I don't like to wear him out. He's just showed me he's all ready for Saturday."

"If you're sure you don't need us, Dawson and I are going to head out on that trail ride."

"Have fun. And thanks again for your help." Dawson took Hunter on a short ride to cool down, then he led him into the barn for a shower and a good brushing. It was nice using facilities in a ranch as well appointed as the Circle C. They had a beautiful washing stall. Made everything so easy. After checking Hunter's hooves, Dawson led him into another stall for brushing. Through the open barn door he could see Sage and Dawson mounting a couple of gleaming chestnut quarter horses. And then they were off, loping toward the open range.

An image of him and Amy doing the same thing came to mind. A pipe dream. This time next week he'd be in Wyoming, and after that California.

Chet finished off the day giving the horses a good feed of alfalfa and protein dry mix. Then he cleaned all his tack. He wasn't ready to leave the ranch until almost seven thirty. The Carrigans were having another barbecue. This time Callan sent her five-year-old daughter to invite him. Little Amelia was petite, but full of confidence, not at all shy.

"Mom and Dad say you should come have some barbecued chicken. It's real good. You can have a drumstick if you want."

"That's a nice offer. Thanks, Amelia, but I've got to get going."

"Why?" Amelia asked with a child-like frankness. "There's blueberry pie for dessert. And ice cream."

Why indeed? thought Chet. Maybe, this once, he should make an exception. The food smelled so damn good, and this kid didn't seem like she was going to take no for an answer anyway. He was about to accept the invitation, when he saw a trail of dust on the approach from the highway. A pickup truck was heading this way. A few seconds later, his heart sank.

He could already hear the muffler. That was his father's truck. Weariness hit him then, the bone-deep kind that felt like it would never end.

"You head on back to the house," he told Amelia. No way did he want her meeting his father. Especially if the old man had been drinking. "Tell your folks thanks. Maybe next time."

He watched to make sure Amelia was doing as he'd asked, before he headed toward his dad's old Dodge. The old man had skidded to a stop and was starting to get out of the cab.

"Stop right there." Chet reached out to prevent the driver's door from opening all the way. "What are you doing here?"

His father looked rough, with a three-day beard and watery eyes. His hand on the door handle had a slight shake. "Been waiting for you to buy me dinner. Thought I'd drive out here and see what was taking so long."

Chet didn't ask how he'd known where Chet was or how to get to the Circle C. A few questions at the Wolf Den would have given Walt all the information he needed.

"You been drinking?" Chet couldn't tell if it was old beer he was smelling or new.

"Not today. Been resting, mostly. Watching TV in that luxury motel you put me up in."

"Beggars can't be choosers. Get back in your truck and follow me. We'll grab something at the Wolf Den."

AMY WAS THINKING that David Wilcox was going to be a no-show when finally, at nine o'clock, she heard the bell on the front door ring. Leaving the towels she'd been folding, she headed toward the foyer, heart racing, palms tingling with nerves.

Standing by the front door was a tall, substantial man with short, mostly gray hair and a craggy, but kind-looking face. He was wearing jeans and a western shirt and was holding his hat in one hand, a duffel bag in the other.

"Welcome. You must be David Wilcox."

"Sure am, little lady."

"Please call me Amy. Do you mind signing the register?" She set a pen out for him, then opened the drawer with the keys.

As he signed, he said, "Real glad you have a room for me. Been planning to attend the rodeo for months but forgot the little matter of reserving a place to stay. My wife says it's because I expected her to do it and she's probably right."

"I'm glad it worked out." She smiled at him, feeling a jolt as she met his light blue, round-shaped eyes. "Let me show you your room. Can I carry your bag for you, Mr. Wilcox?"

"Absolutely not," he said with a smile and a wink. "I'm not that old, yet. And by the way, you can call me D. W. Most folks do."

He followed her up the stairs to the landing and she unlocked the door to the White room. "Queen bed, with an en suite shower and toilet. In the sitting room downstairs you'll find coffee, tea, cookies and fruit from three in the afternoon onward. And breakfast is served from eight to nine."

He dropped his bag on the bench by the bed. "I had dinner with my wife before I left, but a cookie and a cup of coffee would be nice. Any chance you have decaf?"

"I was just making a fresh pot."

"Great. I'll be down in a few minutes."

In the kitchen Amy noticed her fingers trembling as she poured the fresh coffee into a carafe. By the time she'd put it on the sitting room sideboard, refreshed the cream and the cookies, D. W. was back.

He glanced around approvingly at the comfy leather furniture arranged around a massive river rock fireplace. "Nice. I bet it's real cozy in the winter when you have a fire going."

"I hope so. I'm relatively new here."

"Oh?"

"I bought the place about a month ago now."

She poured him a coffee and showed him where the cream and sugar were.

"I take it black, thanks. But I'd love one of those cookies." He settled into a large armchair by the front window. "So how is it a young woman like you buys a big old bed-and-breakfast in Montana? I can tell by your accent you're not from here."

Amy perched on the arm of a love seat. She felt weird, like she was acting a part in a play. Part of her wanted to stop with the polite chitchat and tell him everything. But though she was getting a good vibe from him—he seemed like a good-natured, forthright individual—she felt she ought to be cautious.

"You're right. I'm from out east. About a year ago my mother died in a car crash. We were close, and it's been hard without her. I decided I needed a change, a new adventure if you will. So I took the money she'd left me and invested it here." She waved her hand to indicate the house.

"I'm sorry about your mother, but I admire your bravery. I take it you're on your own?"

She nodded. "Yes. My friends back home think I'm crazy to be doing this. But I'm hoping it works out."

"I bet you're going to make a big success of it. You certainly make a good cup of coffee and a delicious cookie." He cocked his head to one side. "I keep getting the feeling we've met before. But if you're from out east I guess that's not likely. You been to Montana before?"

"Nope, first time." She struggled to keep her tone light. She had a strong resemblance to her mother, though their eyes and hair color were different. Could that be why David thought she looked familiar? Nervously she rubbed at her wrist, missing the bracelet she usually wore and wondering if D. W. would have recognized it if she'd kept it on.

Chapter Eleven

THE CLUB SANDWICH and fries he'd just eaten felt like a heavy mass in Chet's stomach and his head was beginning to ache. It was too loud here at the Wolf Den, even though there were fewer patrons than usual. A lot of the regulars and the out-of-towners were probably on Main Street enjoying barbecued burgers and dancing up a storm on the street. Neither of those appealed to Chet. He needed a walk and some fresh air. But his father had just ordered another beer. Chet signaled for the bill. He'd pay for this one but if his dad wanted more, he'd have to buy his own.

"'Member that time I took you to the petting zoo?" Walt asked.

"Yeah." It was one of the few normal family outings the two of them had ever had. They'd made the rounds of the animals and then his father had bought him an ice cream cone. And that was when he'd told Chet that his grandmother had died.

Chet hadn't cared much for ice cream after that.

"I know I wasn't the perfect father. But I tried."

Chet grunted. Maybe there had been a day or two when

Walt had tried. But the other memories, of sleeping in the truck, of scrounging for food, of having to drag his father to the school in whatever town they happened to be living at the time, so he would register him, those memories were so much weightier.

His father cleared his throat and Chet narrowed his eyes. He'd seen his father try to talk himself out of bad situations often enough to know when Walt was nervous. This had to be it then, the appeal for money.

Chet leaned back on his stool and waited.

"I turned sixty-five in January," Walt began. "Qualified for the Medicaid so I decided to go for a checkup. I'd been to doctors before, to get broken bones fixed and the like, but this was my first checkup."

"How did it go?" Chet asked cautiously, not liking the direction this was headed.

"They sent me for tests and more tests. Took almost a month and I was getting nervous. Must be something serious, right? I worried it was cancer but turns out the problem was my kidneys. Acute kidney failure I think they call it."

"That sounds serious."

Walt's shoulders drooped. "Doc says I'll have to start dialysis soon. No more traveling. Get hooked up to machines three times a week. Most of this is covered by Medicaid. Not all."

"That's bad news. Sorry to hear it." Most sons would be

devastated to hear a diagnosis like this from their father. Chet wanted to feel something, at least sad, but he couldn't muster even that. The one thing he could offer was money. "You need some cash to help with the bills?"

"Yeah. That's part of it."

"There's more?" Chet tensed as once again the conversation took an ominous turn. He turned to face his father, who was staring into his beer like the froth could tell his future.

"Doc says I have a better option than dialysis."

"Oh?"

Walt cleared his throat. "Kidney transplant." Finally he turned to look Chet in the eyes. "All I need is to find a donor."

"Tell me about you," Amy asked her guest. "I read in the rodeo weekend program that you're in the Pro Rodeo Hall of Fame?"

"Yeah, I guess that's proof of how old I am," D. W. said. "Those years I spent on the circuit were crazy, but they sure were fun. Put that all behind me when my sons told me they'd rather go fly-fishing than ride a bucking bronc. Guess they've got a lot more sense than their old man."

"Do your sons live near you?"

"Yup. Two are still at home and the oldest lives with his girlfriend just a few miles away. They all work on our ranch—it's a big operation. I'm grateful they feel the same connection to it that I do. And my wife is glad they still like coming round for Sunday dinners."

Amy wondered about those sons. Her half brothers, maybe. She was curious about the ranch too. And his wife. She wanted to ask to see pictures, longed to pepper him with more questions. Most of all she wanted to know if he remembered her mother. Did he know Helen had given birth to a daughter and if so, what had been his thought process when he decided not to be a part of her life?

But much as she longed to hear those answers, she was also afraid to hear them.

It was probably smarter to wait anyway. D. W. would be here for two nights. There would be other opportunities to talk.

"Sounds like you have a very full and happy life," she said.

"I've been blessed, that's for sure."

She stood. "It's been nice chatting with you. I have a few things to take care of in the kitchen. If you need anything, just come back and find me."

"I'm sure I'll be fine. Thanks for everything, Amy."

In the kitchen Amy tried to chop veggies for a breakfast hash, but her fingers were trembling too much. She opened the screen door and stepped outside. She could hear the distant sound of country music—the street dancing must be in full swing. She wondered if Chet would be there. There was no light in the room above the garage, and his truck was gone.

She desperately wanted to talk to Chet right now. To tell him everything that had just happened and to ask what he thought she should do next.

When should she tell D. W. about her mother? And how should she broach the subject?

In the faint light of the moon, aided by nearby streetlamps, she followed the path along the side of the house until she reached the front porch. She perched on the steps and gazed out toward the mountains. She could hear the burble of the river and though it was too dark to see the mountains, she could feel their presence.

She'd been so uptight all day, it was good to finally take a deep breath and relax. She told herself that was all she was doing out here. Decompressing after a stressful day. But when she saw the old Ford drive up and park, she knew she'd been fooling herself.

She'd been waiting for Chet.

CHET WAS STILL in shock when he arrived at Bramble House after dropping his father off at the motel. Walt had had too much to drink to drive himself. He'd have to walk to the Wolf Den in the morning to get his truck. The walking would be good for him. As would a new diet. What was the old man doing, still drinking and subsisting on burgers and fried foods when his kidneys were failing?

Chet knew he hadn't yet fully processed his conversation with his father. Right now he was too damn tired. He could hear the band playing on Main Street as he got out of his truck, and he thought about all those people dancing and having fun while he hardly had the energy to crawl up the stairs and drag himself into bed.

And then he noticed Amy sitting on her front stairs, and a jolt of adrenaline rushed through him, pushing away the fatigue. He had nothing to offer her, now even less than before, but she was looking in his direction and he automatically started walking toward her.

She made room for him to sit beside her on the step.

"You look tired," she said.

She was probably tired too, but she didn't look it. She looked gorgeous. Her blonde hair glowed in the faint porch light and her eyes looked bluer than ever. He had to force himself to stop staring.

"I am tired," he admitted. "It's been a hell of a day."

"For me too."

And then he remembered. Her father had been scheduled to book in today. "Did David Wilcox show up?"

"Not until after nine, but yes, he did."

"And what did you think?"

"He seems nice. Solid."

"Like you pictured?"

She wrapped her arms around her legs, rested her chin on her knees. "Not at all. As a kid I imagined my father would be like the dad in *To Kill a Mockingbird*. It was my grandparents' favorite movie and we watched it every year. To me Atticus Finch—dark-haired and elegant, intellectual and cultured—was basically the male equivalent of my mother."

"Doesn't sound like David Wilcox."

Amy laughed. "No. He's the total opposite. Earthy and practical and totally unpretentious." She hesitated then added, "It's like discovering you have a whole other side of yourself. I've always related so completely to my mother. And now I find out my father is a rancher, a former rodeo competitor. It's blowing my mind."

"Does he know he's your father?"

"No. I didn't say anything yet. But there was this moment when he told me I looked familiar. I wondered if he was noticing my resemblance to my mother. I almost said something then. But I chickened out."

"What scares you most about telling him?"

"So many things. What if he rejects me? What if he doesn't believe me? Maybe what would be hardest is if I've connected the dots wrong and he isn't really my father after all. Then I'd be back to square one with no idea where to look next."

He wanted so badly to put an arm around her shoulders and pull her close for a hug. But he knew that if he touched her, he wouldn't be able to stop at a hug. "Hey, if you don't find your father, I'd be happy to give you mine."

She bumped her shoulder against his. "No thanks."

"Yeah, I don't blame you."

She turned to face him, her eyes thoughtful. "How is Walt? Has he asked you for money yet or do you think he's going to wait to see if you win at the rodeo?"

"Funny you should ask. We had one of our longer conversations this evening at the Wolf Den—not a place I'd recommend, by the way—and he finally told me why he wanted to see me."

"Not money?"

"Not entirely money. He's got some sort of kidney disease."

"Can it be treated?"

"Dialysis is an option." He hesitated, then took a deep breath. "So is finding a kidney donor."

Amy blinked. Then she sat tall. "He can't—He wouldn't dare—Please tell me he isn't asking you to donate one of yours?"

He was relieved to see she found the idea as preposterous as it had first seemed to him. "Only my old man would have the nerve. But yeah. That's what he's asking."

"What's the procedure? Would you have to be vetted? And gosh, what kind of outcome can he expect at his age, with his drinking?"

"I don't know the answer to any of those questions. The old man is pretty vague about the entire business. I'm going to have to go see his doctor and find out for myself."

"You say that like you intend to do it."

He nodded. He hadn't realized himself, until this very moment. "Believe me, a large part of me wants to tell him to go to hell. But I don't think I could live with myself unless I at least made the effort to get the facts. If my kidney could make a real difference…how do I say no?"

"Oh, Chet."

She was looking at him like she had the other night, when he hadn't been able to stop himself from kissing her. So he had to turn away. To stare out at the sky and try to make that part of himself, the part that sometimes hoped he could be a regular guy, with a regular life, go dead.

"If roles were reversed…would your father do it for you? Give you one of his kidneys?"

He snorted. "I wouldn't want one of Walt's kidneys."

"Assuming they were healthy kidneys, though. Would he?"

Chet didn't need to think long. "Probably not. But that's not the point, is it? If I went through life holding myself to my father's standards, what sort of man would I be?"

Chapter Twelve

D. W. WAS first down for breakfast the next morning. As Amy set out the overnight French toast and crispy bacon—Carol's method had worked like a charm—she asked if he was ready to watch the parade that morning.

"Not just watch. I'm in it, along with some other local hall-of-famers."

"That's so cool. Who else will be in the parade? Are there many floats?"

"Sure there'll be some floats sponsored by local businesses, but mostly you'll see lots of horses, marching bands, local tribe members in traditional ceremonial dress, old-fashioned tractors, cars and maybe a fire engine. Basically a kaleidoscope of all the people and traditions that helped fashion the old west into what it is today."

"That sounds pretty interesting."

"If you've never seen one before you shouldn't miss it. The one here in Marietta starts on Main Street then makes its way to the fairgrounds. Just find a spot to stand—better yet bring a folding chair with you—somewhere along the route and you'll be set."

"Thanks. I will try to make it."

"You said last night you were from out east?"

She could feel her heart start to pound hard in her chest. "Yes."

"Where in particular?"

"New York City." She straightened the cutlery on the table, telling herself that it was a normal question he was asking. He couldn't possibly suspect who she really was.

"I knew this girl from New York once," he said.

There it was, Amy thought. The perfect opening for her to mention her mother. But she didn't. Instead she offered D. W. a refill of his coffee.

"Don't mind if I do." He held out his mug. "You do have tickets to the rodeo, right?"

"Well…rodeos aren't really my thing, D. W."

He shook his head. "I don't believe this. Amy, this is your first summer in Montana. You have got to go to the rodeo. That's the only way to appreciate the artistry and the skill of cowboys and cowgirls. Tell you what. I have an extra ticket—bought it for my wife before she told me she wasn't coming. Meet me at the fairgrounds and we'll go together."

Realistically Amy knew she didn't have time to go to the parade or the rodeo. But this was a chance to spend time with her father. There was no way she could turn him down.

"That's very kind of you. Thanks, I'd love to come."

"One condition," D. W. said. He pointed at the slip-on sandals she was wearing. "You have to get a pair of cowboy boots. And a hat. There's a western wear shop on Main Street. You live in Marietta, you need the right duds.

AMY COULDN'T REMEMBER the last time she'd gone shopping for clothes so she figured she was due a little retail therapy. Joanie, the manager at Marietta Western Wear, was helpful. *Too* helpful. Amy went into the change room with an embroidered top, but Joanie kept passing her items in the change stall and she ended up with a flared skirt and a beautifully tooled western belt as well. The addition of boots and hat completed the outfit.

She stared at her reflection. Who was this woman? She wished she could text a photo to her mother. *Look at me, Mom! I've gone country!*

She put the photo on the Bramble House Insta account instead. Eliza had usually posted about twice a week but though this was a job she'd normally enjoy Amy had only posted twice since taking ownership. No wonder she felt like such a failure. She *was* failing.

But for this afternoon, she wasn't going to worry about it. She was going to her first rodeo. With her father. How crazy was that?

D. W. had told her to meet him at the entrance to the fairground and when she arrived, he was there, waiting. His face lit up when he saw her.

"Don't you look great! Now you're getting into the spirit. How about we grab a corn dog and a lemonade before we take our seats?"

It had been at least a decade since her last corn dog, and she had forgotten how totally yummy they were.

"The secret is lots of mustard," D. W. said. "But be careful not to get any on those pretty new clothes."

As they made their way to their places in the bleachers, many people called hello to D. W. and he nodded and smiled, sometimes stopping to chat or trade good-natured insults. Amy watched the exchanges with a sense of incredulity. This man, she was now ninety-five percent certain, was her father.

Her father.

She'd come to Montana hoping to find him, but not really believing it would happen. Twenty-six years was a long time. People moved. People died. Yet here he was, close enough for her to touch.

"Our seats are here," D. W. said, indicating a bench just a few rows up from the fenced-in ring. He waited for Amy to sit first, before settling beside her.

"We're nice and close to the action," D. W. said. "See those boxes? Those are called chutes. That's where the crew are going to load the bucking horses and bulls."

"Really? That close?" She'd almost be able to touch them.

"Sure is exciting, huh?"

That was one word for it. Amy wasn't sure how she was going to feel once the actual rodeo events started. But there was no denying the anticipation and crackling energy in the air. She wondered where Chet was right now. Was he feeling nervous?

"Hey, Amy," someone called from behind her. Amy turned and saw Sage, sitting in the next row with three other women.

"I didn't know you knew D. W.," Sage said.

"He's a guest at the B & B."

D. W. twisted around and shook Sage's hand. "Nice to see you, Sage. Been a lot of years."

"That's the truth. These are my sisters. Callan and her husband took over the family ranch after my dad died. Mattie breeds Tennessee walkers in the Flathead Valley and the brainy one at the end of the row is Dani, the academic in the family."

An explosion of fireworks truncated the conversation.

Amy turned to face the arena as the national anthem began to play. Then three young women came out on horses, circling the arena and waving at the crowd.

"Give a big welcome to the Copper Mountain Rodeo Queen, Miss Lindsay Cotter."

Amy took a moment to appreciate the woman's horsemanship as well as that of the other two women in the ring with her, before turning to the program in her lap. Quickly she flipped the pages, anxious to see when the tie-roping event would start. She couldn't know how Chet was doing, but her stomach was churning, making her regret the corn dog and the mustard. She didn't care if he won or not, she just didn't want to see him get hurt. Not him or any of the other cowboys or the animals.

She scanned the folks hanging out around the perimeter of the arena. Most were fit young men, dressed similarly, their faces partially obscured by their iconic cowboy hats. Among the cameramen she spotted Rick, wearing headphones and catching some of the behind-the-scenes action for the documentary.

But she couldn't find Chet.

"You ever been on a cattle ranch, Amy?"

She refocused her attention on D. W. "No, I haven't."

"That's too bad. Cause the cattle ranch is where rodeoing started. All the skills you're going to see on display today are skills a wrangler needs when he or she is working with cattle."

Obviously he was proud of his heritage. "What's your ranch called? Has it been in your family long?"

"My great-grandfather settled Whispering Pines in the late eighteen hundreds. Our family has always believed that we are not owners of the land, but stewards. There's a revolution going on in ranching today, trying to make it more sustainable and eco-friendly. But that's a tune my family's been playing for a very long time."

Amy couldn't speak for a moment. The man he spoke of

as his great-grandfather would have been her great-great-grandfather. D. W. didn't know it yet, but his family was also her family. And suddenly it was hitting her hard all she had missed. The heritage she'd grown up knowing nothing about. Yes, she'd had a happy childhood, but for the first time she questioned whether it had been enough.

How might her life have changed if D. W. had been in the picture? Conceivably she'd have spent part of her summer with him, on the ranch. She'd have had the benefit of his guidance as well as her mother's. She'd have grown up knowing her half brothers, riding horses, learning the ins and outs of the cattle ranching business firsthand.

Why hadn't any of that happened? Was it her mother's fault for not trying hard enough to find her father? Or was it D. W.'s? Had he known about her all along but made the choice not to be a part of her life?

All of these questions were swirling and churning inside her. She felt like she would go crazy if she didn't get answers soon. Now.

But they were in the middle of a rodeo.

And suddenly the announcer's voice cut through her ruminations.

"...Chet Hardwick from Boulder, Colorado. Chet's one of the world's best and this is his first time in Marietta. How about it folks, can we give Chet a Montana-sized welcome?"

Amy joined the clapping belatedly but enthusiastically. She could see Chet now, mounted on Hunter, waiting to compete. She couldn't believe she'd zoned out like that. Chet was fifth of ten competitors. She'd missed the first four cowboys.

"Thought maybe you were sleeping with your eyes wide open," D. W. teased. "Glad you woke up for this fellow. Tie-down roping is the most technical event in the rodeo, and this is the guy to watch, if you ask me."

"Chet is staying at Bramble House in the room over the garage. Do you know him?"

"Never had the pleasure of meeting him, but I knew his dad. Nasty fellow that Walt Hardwick."

Amy glanced quickly at D. W. "I've heard he had a drinking problem."

"*Has* a drinking problem," D. W. corrected. "A problem with his temper too. Chet deserved far better. It's amazing how well he's turned out with a father like that. I'd really like the chance to meet him. He's staying at Bramble House you say?"

"Yes, though he's away a lot, looking after his horses."

D. W.'s eyes were on the action in the ring. "Looks like Chet is in position. Let me tell you what to watch for…"

As D. W. explained the complex rules of tie-down roping, Amy stayed focused on Chet and his horse. Once Chet gave the signal, he was ready, it all happened so fast, she could hardly follow the action. But by the way the crowd—and D. W. and Sage—hooted and cheered she guessed it had gone well for Chet.

"And what a time!" said the announcer. "The man from Boulder should be mighty proud. Six point nine seconds, folks. Don't come much faster than that."

"So he did good?" she asked D. W.

He laughed. "Oh, yeah. Better than good. I feel sorry for the poor fellas who have to follow him."

As Chet waved to the crowd, acknowledging their cheers, Amy was certain he spotted her. She saw his smile broaden and knew she was beaming too. She couldn't help herself.

D. W. must have noticed. "Yup he's a good man. Works hard and has a level head on his shoulders. I've heard he's helped a lot of young cowboys learn to set aside money so they have something concrete to show for their years on the rodeo. If anyone deserves to win his event, it's Chet."

As it turned out, none of the guys after Chet were able to match his time. Amy shot him a quick text message of congratulations, and then the barrel racers were up. When Ruby Lancaster's turn came, her parents, seated several sections away, hollered and clapped for their daughter, clearly overcome with pride.

Ruby's short curly red hair was barely visible under her black cowboy hat. As she shot out from the gate and rounded her first barrel Amy had a glimpse of a round, pretty face, features set with focused determination.

"Nice time," D. W. said when the announcer gave Ruby's score. "But the competitor to watch is local girl, Willow McBride."

Amy saw what he meant when, two competitors later, Willow raced into the ring, her long hair streaming behind her as she made fast, tight turns around all three barrels.

"Wow," Amy said. She couldn't believe the speed and control and the obvious connection these competitors had with their horses. More than ever she was inspired to continue with her riding lessons. Not that she expected to ever be able to acquire the skill of these riders. But it would be fun to try.

Bulldogging was next, and while Amy tried to focus on the action and D. W.'s helpful commentary, she kept scanning the crowds, looking for Chet. He hadn't responded to her text. Probably he was too busy. She hoped he was enjoying his moment of fame. When she did finally spot him, she almost wished she hadn't.

His father was with him.

Amy had no idea what they were talking about but Chet's body language—shoulders stooped, head downcast—told the story. At a time when Chet ought to be feeling on top of the world, his father was making him miserable.

She was beginning to really hate Walt Hardwick.

Chapter Thirteen

AFTER THE DAY'S rodeo events were concluded, people stood and stretched and left the bleachers to gather around the kiosks selling beer and popcorn, ice cream and mini donuts. Amy stuck with D. W. at first but he couldn't get more than a few steps before someone new came to shake his hand and tell him about the time they saw him compete at the Last Stand in Coulee City, at the Darby Xtreme, at the Little Big Horn Stampede…the list of rodeos, the numbers of people, it was all overwhelming.

Amy managed to thank D. W. for the tickets, then slip away. The conversation she needed to have with him had to happen someplace quiet and private. Probably at the B & B. Maybe later tonight. The thought made her palms sweat. So she tried to distract herself by scanning the crowd. Maybe she could chat with Sage and get to know her sisters a little. Sage with her height and her gorgeous red hair was easy to find but just like D. W., the Carrigans were swarmed by friends and neighbors who wanted to chat.

For a while Amy people-watched. Then she wandered to the line-up for mini donuts.

If she lived here long enough, would she eventually have lots of friends too? Or would she always be the woman who didn't quite fit in? Even when she tried to dress the part?

"So, the New York girl likes donuts."

She recognized Chet's voice even before she turned around to see the man himself. She put a finger on her lips. "Don't tell anyone. I'm supposed to be loyal to bagels and pretzels but I really prefer donuts." Then she threw her arms around his neck. "You were fabulous today. Congratulations!"

He stiffened under her hug, but then he squeezed her back. "Thanks, Amy. Everything just clicked today."

"You sure looked impressive. Not that I understand much about the rules, though D. W. did try to explain them."

"I noticed you two were sitting together."

"He had an extra ticket he'd bought for his wife."

Chet raised his eyebrows. "Well? Did you talk?"

"Not about my mother, or any of that. I'm still trying to find the right moment. It certainly wasn't here at the rodeo. He can't take three steps without someone stepping up to shake his hand."

"He's earned a lot of respect. Not just for what he did in the ring, but for the work he's done to help underprivileged kids. He's just an all-around good guy. You should be proud that he's your father."

"I guess I'm still in a state of shock about the whole

thing. It doesn't feel real. I kept pinching myself at the rodeo. It felt like a dream."

"Interesting that he asked you to go with him. Do you think he suspects?"

She considered the idea and dismissed it. "No. He just thought this city slicker needed some educating about the rodeo."

"Not a city slicker anymore I see." Chet stepped back to admire her outfit. "The new look suits you."

She twirled, making her skirt flare. "I went a bit overboard. But I made sure to buy practical boots I can use for my next riding lesson and not the pretty turquoise ones that first caught my eye."

He checked out her boots. "That's a good brand. They'll last a long time."

His voice suddenly seemed flat to her. "What's wrong?"

"I'm wishing I could be the person who gives you your next lesson."

She wanted to say he could be. But then she remembered. Tomorrow was Sunday. After the rodeo finals, he'd be off to the next town. "So where's your father?"

"He ran into some old pals of his. I'm guessing they're at the beer garden. Or the Wolf Den on Front Street."

She'd heard of that bar. Mostly as a place to avoid.

"What would you like, miss?"

They'd reached the front of the donut line. Amy requested a small bag for them to share, and before she could pay,

Chet had done it.

"You didn't have to do that."

"Hey, I'm on my way to winning a ten-thousand-dollar purse. I guess I can afford five dollars of donuts."

She popped one into her mouth, then did the same for Chet. Their gazes locked as her fingers brushed his lips.

"Is there anything as delicious as deep-fried dough covered in cinnamon sugar?" she asked.

"I can think of one thing."

Yes. So could she. "So now what?" she asked.

"Guess we follow the crowds back to the park in front of the courthouse. That's where the steak dinner will be happening."

Amy checked her watch and was surprised to see it was almost six. "Oh my Lord. I've got to get back to the B & B. I had no idea it was so late. I didn't put out cookies and coffee at three. Plus about a million other chores that should have been done by now."

"I bet none of your guests missed the cookies. They'll all be here at the rodeo, then the steak dinner. How about you let the work slide for a bit and come to the barbecue with me? I usually skip these things, 'cause I always feel awkward, like I don't belong. It would be great to have your company."

She paused. She could tell it had been hard for him to admit to feeling awkward. Now that she knew him better, she understood that shame about his father lay behind his feeling of not belonging. It was so unfair, but she got it. As the days went by Marietta was growing on her, but she wasn't growing on Marietta. She felt as much the outsider as the day she'd first moved here.

"What the hell." She snugged her arm through his. "You deserve to celebrate tonight. Let's party. And by party I mean drink lemonade and eat steak with all the fixings."

DAYS DIDN'T COME much better than this one, Chet thought, as he and Amy approached Main Street. He had a pretty woman on his arm, the top score of the day at the rodeo, and a delicious steak dinner to look forward to. He and Amy strolled up one side of the street and down the other, admiring the various window displays. All the merchants seemed to be trying to outdo one another with their creative rodeo displays.

"Isn't that amazing." Amy paused, transfixed by the display in the toy store window. A ranch house and barn, corral and loafing sheds, all created with Lego blocks.

Farther on, the antique store had recreated a ranch kitchen from the early nineteen hundreds, with two mannequin cowboys having coffee at the table.

Another country and western band was setting up on the stage for the evening and before long they were playing a cover of Kenny Chesney's "Summertime." Impromptu dancing broke out in front of the courthouse and Chet cocked an eyebrow at Amy.

"You game?"

"Lead on, Cowboy."

He put one hand on the small of her back and clasped her hand with the other. She felt so good in his arms, smelled so good too. Then right there, on the sidewalk, they started dancing. Amy followed his every step beautifully, throwing back her head and laughing when he guided her round in a twirl. One song led to another. And when they finally stopped, he realized a small crowd had gathered around them to watch. As they clapped and cheered he and Amy took bows.

"Wow, you can really dance," Amy said breathlessly, her eyes bright and cheeks pink.

"When you don't drink, going to bars means playing pool or dancing. I've done a lot of both."

"Sounds like a handy skill set."

"Not really. Well, the dancing maybe." And he'd never enjoyed it more than today. "What about you? Where'd you learn to dance like that?"

She threw up her hands. "Me? I was just faking it."

"No wild partying during your college days?"

"I probably should have partied more than I did. My mom was a serious academic and that rubbed off on me. Plus, I needed to keep up my grades for scholarships."

"Does that mean no time for guys either?" He kept his

tone light, but he was probably more interested in her answer than he had a right to be.

"I had the same boyfriend throughout my undergrad degree. Eventually we realized we were better as friends than lovers. Since Scott, I've only dated casually. What about you?"

"Moving around the way I do, it's never been good for relationships of any sort. Especially not with women."

"Other cowboys manage to have relationships," she observed. "It's more than the moving around for you, isn't it?"

She wouldn't let him get away with the pat answer. They were getting to know each other well. Too well. It made Chet uncomfortable to realize how much he'd revealed of himself to this woman. Yet he couldn't seem to stop himself.

He could make some excuse and walk away right now, for instance.

In the long run it would be the kinder thing to do. But he didn't have the willpower. He wanted every minute of Amy's time that he could have.

"I'm a loner. Always been that way."

"Always? Or just since your grandmother died and you went to live with your father?"

"A lot of things changed at that point. No doubt I did too."

Amy put her hand on his arm. "I saw your father talking to you at the rodeo this afternoon. You looked pretty unhappy."

"Most conversations with Walt make me unhappy." That was putting it lightly. Most conversations with Walt made him feel like a worthless piece of trash. Even now as an adult, with all he'd accomplished, Walt still had that power. Chet didn't understand it. He only wished he could find a way out from the burden of being Walt Hardwick's son.

"Was he pressuring you for your kidney again?"

"He's already won that battle. No, he was critiquing my performance in the ring. Like I need any guidance from him," Chet added bitterly. His father had never done as well in the rodeo as he had. Yet he talked as if he was some venerable hall-of-famer.

"D. W. said you were the man to watch, and he was right. Most fathers would have been proud to see their son do as well as you did."

"Yeah, well Walt has never been like most fathers."

He was moved by the way Amy looked at him. With compassion, not pity. And yeah, he knew the difference. Now she reached out and touched his arm, something he noticed she did a lot.

"Did Walt help you with anything when you were growing up? Teach you to ride? Or how to throw a rope?"

"Walt taught me nothing. Mostly I just watched and mimicked the other cowboys. Some of them took pity on me and gave me pointers."

"He sounds so despicable. It makes me sick to think of you giving up one of your kidneys to help that man."

It made him feel a little sick too. But he couldn't see he had a choice. "Enough about Walt. I thought we were out for some fun tonight. Doesn't that barbecue smell great? Let's get in line."

Amy laughed and shook her head. "Okay, Chet, we won't talk about serious stuff anymore."

They joined the queue and filled their plates with steaks that were almost two inches thick, baked potatoes, and salads, then found a quiet place in the shade of an old oak tree.

"I can't remember the last time I had a steak," Amy said. "I have to admit this is pretty tasty."

"Sure is." But though he was plenty hungry, after a few bites Chet found he'd rather watch Amy than eat.

"Stop looking at me," she said. "You're making me self-conscious."

"Aw, don't spoil my fun, Amy. Two days from now I'll still be able to eat steak." But two days from now he would no longer be able to look at her.

She stopped chewing and gave him a poignant look. "So you're still set on leaving Sunday after finals?"

"That's the plan."

"And what happens after that?"

"I've got competitions in Wyoming and California. After that, I'm not sure. It'll depend on my standings, I suppose, but I almost don't care how I do. I think I've had enough of the rodeo lifestyle. I'd like to settle down, but I'm not sure what to do."

"Sage and D. W. both mentioned that you have a skill for financial planning."

"Yeah, I'm thinking about that. I do have my degree. And I get a lot of satisfaction helping my colleagues who may not be as financially literate. But I'm not sure if that'll be a good career fit for me in the long run."

Amy looked at his plate. "You're really not going to finish that?"

"Nope."

"Then how about we go back to Bramble House and watch our last sunset together?"

LAST SUNSET TOGETHER. The weight of those words stayed with Amy as she and Chet wandered back to the B & B. She'd tucked her hand around his arm again. She liked the feel of his solid body next to hers. Such a strong, self-reliant man, and yet his father still held such power over him. She'd been lucky to have a mother who was kind and encouraging, the very opposite of Chet's dad.

She wished she could phone her mother tonight and tell her about Chet. How special he was, how talented and honorable. Maybe her mother would have had some advice. How to convince Chet to stay? Or maybe how to forget him when he left? Then again, maybe her mother wouldn't have been much help, since she clearly hadn't forgotten about D. W. Not judging by the way she'd cherished his bracelet. D. W. might very well be the reason her mother had stayed single all those years, as well.

Something else Amy wished she could talk to her mother about.

These were regrets she was going to have to live with. But right now she was too focused on the man beside her. She wanted to be fully present for the moments that were left to them.

When they arrived at the B & B the sky was a beautiful periwinkle blue, streaked with wispy apricot clouds. Amy ran inside for a quick check of the sitting room. Cookie platter was empty. Fruit bowl was empty. Water pitchers and tea and coffee thermoses, also empty.

"I should put out some refreshments for when my guests get back from the steak dinner."

"They'll be too full to want anything." Chet had followed her inside. Now he put a hand on her shoulder. "Let's just sit and enjoy the sunset for a bit."

They sat in chairs, side by side. Chet moved his leg so his knee touched hers. When she glanced at him, he smiled.

"I can't get over how pretty you look wearing a cowboy hat."

She laughed. "I forgot I was even wearing it."

"Funny how fast you can get used to something." Chet leaned over and removed her hat, setting it upside down on the porch railing. Then he gently finger-combed her hair, bringing back the spring to her curls.

His touch sent tingles down her neck and spine. She met his gaze and willed him to kiss her.

He took his time, bathing each of her features in the warm glow of his obvious admiration, before he finally dipped his head and kissed her gently but lingeringly.

They had come out here to enjoy the sunset, but neither of them noticed the shades of violet and rose, teal and indigo that must have paraded over the sky before it finally grew dark.

Amy placed her hand on the side of his face. She wanted to remember the up-close angle of his cheekbones, the warmth of his eyes, the curve of his bottom lip. Would she see him again? She knew better than to ask for promises.

Even though she really wanted one.

"I don't want you to go."

Chet placed his hand over hers and gently brought it down to his thigh where he sandwiched it with his other hand. "I'll never forget this week. And to think I didn't want to stay at Bramble House. Thank you for having that no-last-minute-cancellation policy."

Chapter Fourteen

It was possible that despite their better intentions, she and Chet would have ended up sharing a room that night. But the band had stopped playing after sunset and now the other B & B guests began to return. The Lancasters were first. Before they even made it to the porch steps, Chet was squeezing her arm and whispering good night.

He nodded to the Lancasters but didn't break stride on his way to the room above the garage.

"Is that the fellow who won the tie-down today?" Fred asked as he and his wife joined Amy on the porch.

"Yes. Chet Hardwick."

"I didn't realize he was staying here," Sue said. "He hasn't been down for breakfast."

"He's up early to see to his horses. He's been boarding them at a local ranch." Amy opened the door to usher them inside. Now that Chet was gone the night air had begun to feel cool. "Ruby did great today. You must be so pleased."

"Yes, it was a personal best for her," Fred said, chest expanding with pride. "Too bad she faced such stiff competition from Willow McBride."

"Ruby's still young," her mother said. "She'll give Willow a run for her money one of these days."

"I'd say she did that today," Amy said. She noticed the Lancasters gazing at the depleted side table. "Sorry I didn't get tea out this afternoon. Can I get you something now? A cookie or a piece of fruit? Maybe tea or coffee?"

"We ate so much at the steak dinner I think we'll just head up to our room," Fred said. "It's been a long day and we have to rest up for tomorrow."

"Are you planning to go to the pancake breakfast?" Amy asked hopefully.

"Sure are. We're meeting Ruby there."

"Great. Well, I'll have coffee and muffins down here to tide you over if you're up early."

"Perfect. Good night, Amy." The middle-aged couple made their way to Mable's suite on the main floor.

As soon as they were gone, Amy hastily put out some packaged cookies and hot water for tea. She was about to brew a pot of decaf when the doc crew came in next. They looked wiped, but triumphant.

"Got some great footage today," Rick told her, grabbing a handful of cookies before heading for the stairs. "But now I'm ready to crash."

Lucy and Graham weren't in such a hurry to retire. "I'd love some herbal tea if it isn't too much trouble," Lucy said.

"Same," Graham added.

"Just boiled some water. What type of tea would you

like?"

When they both asked for peppermint, she pulled out the packets and added the tea bags to the hot water.

"Thanks, Amy." Lucy relaxed on one of the sofas. "Were you at the rodeo? We didn't see you."

"I was there. You were probably too busy to notice me."

"We did get some great interviews," Graham said. "My favorite was the barrel racer Willow McBride. I can't imagine how she was able to focus in the rodeo ring with all that's been going on with her."

"You mean the wedding?" Amy guessed.

"I mean *canceling* the wedding," Graham said.

"Really?"

Lucy laughed. "Yes, really. It's been an amazing week for us. So much drama. Our only disappointment was not getting an interview with Chet Hardwick. I've heard he grew up on the circuit, watching his father compete. I bet he'd have some wonderful stories, but every time we get close to him, he manages to elude us."

Amy wondered what Lucy and Graham would say if they knew Chet was staying here at the B & B. Not that she was about to tell them. "I've heard he's a private man," she said.

"Yes. That's what everyone says," Graham agreed. "Which only makes me more determined to land that interview."

The front door opened then and in came her last guest. Amy went to greet D. W. with a vague idea that this might be a good time to have their talk. But D. W. was done for the night.

"I'm beat, gonna head up to my room. I've got another spare ticket for the rodeo tomorrow, Amy, if you want it." He took the ticket from his wallet and handed it to her.

"Thanks, D. W. Will I see you for breakfast or are you going to the pancake fundraiser?"

"Pancake fundraiser for me," D. W. said.

"For us too," Lucy added. "D. W., we still need to get some time with you."

"Get me after my pancakes and bacon," D. W. told them with a wink. "Right now I'm going up to my room and calling my wife."

Amy watched him go, aware that her palms had started sweating again. She couldn't keep up the pretense of being a random B & B owner much longer. She needed to tell D. W. who her mother had been. And find out, for sure, if he was really her father.

Chapter Fifteen

SUNDAY MORNING WAS like a holiday for Amy. All she had to do was make coffee since she and all her guests would be eating at the town's pancake breakfast by the courthouse at the end of Main Street. According to the Bramble House binder, Eliza and Marshall usually volunteered at the event, but Amy was glad no one had signed her up to help. She was looking forward to getting served for a change.

D. W. was the last to join the group seated around the dining room table. Amy poured his coffee and then sat down with her guests to enjoy her third cup of the morning.

She'd gotten up early hoping to catch a few moments with Chet, but he and his truck were already gone by the time she was dressed. Her new outfit needed washing, so she was wearing her normal jeans and a T-shirt today, but she did plan to put on her new boots and hat when she went to the rodeo.

Before leaving her room, she'd tucked a special something into her front pocket. It was today or never. She hoped she didn't lose her nerve.

"So. Finals today," D. W. commented. "Is Ruby nervous?" he asked the Lancasters.

"I think we're more nervous than she is," Sue confessed.

"She gave Willow McBride a run for her money yesterday. I'll be sure to cheer her on today," D. W. said. He leaned back into his chair and took a sip of coffee. "Darn, that is good coffee. I'm going to give your B & B a five-star rating young lady."

"Gosh I'd sure appreciate that. I've only been at this for about a month, but I'm trying."

She noticed the Lancasters exchange a secret glance, while Rick and Graham gazed down into their coffee mugs. Clearly they weren't as impressed as D. W.

"It's a beautiful B & B and I absolutely love Marietta," Lucy said into the void. "And I'm sure that, with more experience, you'll smooth out the rough edges in the service. Perhaps if you hired some help…?"

Amy bit back her gut response. These people did not need to hear the sad story about her entire staff quitting on her first day. Instead she smiled. "I appreciate the feedback. By the way, you're all checking out today, but if you'd like to leave your luggage in your rooms until after the rodeo that's fine with me. I'll just clean around them."

"Thanks, Amy," Lucy said. "That would be great."

"No problem."

Lucy turned to D. W. next. "You still haven't agreed to a time for our interview."

"Like I said last night…" he took a sip of his coffee "…after I have my pancakes and bacon."

"So…ten o'clock?"

He chuckled. "Ma'am, you don't give up."

"Today's our last day of filming and we've got a lot to cover," Lucy said. "Your interview is too important to miss."

"Aw, I'm just an old has-been."

Lucy opened the notebook she always carried with her and flipped a few pages. "According to the Pro Rodeo Hall of Fame website, and I quote: *David Wilcox, or D. W. as he was known as on the circuit, was an elite athlete on a horse and a gentleman off it. While earning success for ten seasons in both bareback riding and saddle-bronc riding, including three National Finals Rodeo Champions and second and third in the Worlds, he is also known for starting up the Big Sky Rodeo Academy for underprivileged kids, a project he and his wife have sponsored for over fifteen years.* End quote."

"Wow," Amy said. She already had a lot of respect for this man—her father—but now she had a deeper appreciation for why so many people had wanted to shake his hand and have a few words.

"If you're going to give some PR for my rodeo schools, then I'm all for doing your interview," D. W. said. "But don't pile the accolades on me. It's the kids who deserve them. Some of their stories would break your heart, yet they still triumph. That's the magic of horses. Other animals, too, but in my biased opinion horses are the best."

"I have to agree," Sue said. "Ruby was the sweetest child until she turned twelve. Suddenly she was rude and argumentative, deliberately disobeying our rules, hanging out with the wrong crowds and skipping classes. Smartest thing we ever did was enroll her in horseback riding lessons."

"I thought it was a damn expensive hobby," Fred added. "Until I saw how it turned Ruby around. She dropped her old friends and made new ones at the stable. Spent all her free time with the horses. When she wasn't riding she was cleaning stalls and grooming the other horses."

Amy suddenly noticed Rick was filming.

"That was great," Amy said. "Can we use that?"

The Lancasters exchanged a glance and then shrugged. "Sure."

"Can't let your guard down around here," D. W. joked. "Now according to my watch it's pancake time."

Everyone got up from the table to put on their boots and hats. Once outside Amy could hear the band warming up. Seconds later they started on a tune Amy knew very well. Her mother had told her it was the inspiration for her name.

D. W. fell into step beside her. "This song brings back memories for me."

Her heart began beating crazily. "Is that right?"

"Yeah, the summer I turned nineteen, I met this girl." He paused and frowned, then gave her a quizzical look. "You said last night you were from out east?"

She rubbed her sweaty palms against her jeans. "Yes."

"New York City?"

"Yes." She kept her gaze forward, telling herself that it was a normal question he was asking. He couldn't possibly suspect who she really was.

"That's where this girl was from—New York City."

There it was, Amy thought. The perfect opening for her to mention her mother. But suddenly they were joined by a neighbor who recognized D. W. and started peppering him with questions. More people were emerging from their homes and joining the procession and Amy lost sight of D. W. and the rest of her guests.

There was too much noise and too many distractions to have a proper conversation anyway, she consoled herself. But time was running out. No more waiting for the right opportunity. Next chance she got, she was telling him. Everything.

A large outdoor tent had been set up on the lawn outside the courthouse. Next to it were several barbecues and a long table where volunteers were flipping pancakes. Among them Amy recognized Sage. The tall cowboy beside her must be her husband.

Traffic had been closed for several blocks on Main Street, making room for rows and rows of tables and chairs. The number of people attending blew Amy's mind. She'd never seen so many good-looking cowboys, or attractive women, not to mention children of all ages, including babes in arms.

Amy had attended lots of outdoor festivals in New York, and while they had all been fun and made her feel proud of her city, the atmosphere in this town was different. The people here smiled more. Not just at their family and friends, but at complete strangers too.

Like her.

And almost without exception they were dressed for the rodeo. Jeans, leather belts, boots and western shirts. Some of the women wore flared skirts and beautiful southwestern-style jewelry. She saw chunky silver and turquoise necklaces, beautifully beaded dangling earrings, and lots of silver bangles.

People here were proud of their western heritage. And not afraid to show it.

The band had been set up on a stage near the center of the action. One song ended and another started and soon half the people in the crowd were singing, "She had me at heads Carolina…"

Amy didn't follow the country music scene, but even she knew these lyrics and she joined in the chorus as she lined up for breakfast. Suddenly she felt a hand on her elbow. Turning, she saw it was Chet. He was smiling at her, approvingly. "Country and western, huh? I would have pegged you for a Taylor Swift fan."

"I'm that too, but I have to admit this music is infectious." She waved a hand at the crowd. "I thought the pancake breakfast was going to be lame, but the community spirit here is incredible."

"And wait until you taste the pancakes."

He seemed in a much better mood this morning, and frankly so was she. Maybe it was the celebratory air and the sunshine combining to push all their problems to the background.

They grabbed plates and cutlery first, then were served bacon and sausages and finally pancakes. It was Sage who piled up first Amy's plate, then Chet's.

"Welcome to your first Marietta rodeo weekend, Amy," Sage said. "I'd like you to meet my husband Dawson."

Dawson smiled at Amy then turned to Chet. "Good luck this afternoon, buddy. We'll be rooting for you."

"Will you be competing too?" Amy asked Dawson.

"Hell no. I hung up my spurs years ago."

"Ten years ago to be exact," Sage said. "When he asked me to marry him."

"I won All-Around that year," Dawson said. "And she still almost turned me down."

Laughing, Amy and Chet moved down the line to the platters of fruit. Carol Bingley was serving here, handing out thick slices of juicy locally grown melons. Amy said thanks and hurried along, before Carol could find something new to lecture her about.

Chet found them a couple of spots at a table and as they sat down to eat, she remarked, "Sage and Dawson seem like a fun couple."

"They're good people. I really missed them when they left the rodeo circuit. You should have seen Sage race the barrels. She was unstoppable back then. Until she injured her knee."

"That's a shame."

"I think her dad was more disappointed than she was. Sage found her true calling when she started making chocolates."

Amy wondered if the B & B would turn out to be her true calling. So far it felt a lot more like a big mistake. "Do you think financial planning could be your true calling, Chet?"

"Maybe. The idea of starting up a business appeals to me. But I'm not sure about spending my days cooped up in an office."

"There have to be other options out there. You'll think of something."

"Excuse me, folks." A gorgeous lady dressed in stylish western wear had commandeered the mike from the band. Everyone turned to look as she introduced herself.

"For those who don't know me I'm Chelsea Collier Flint, your mayor."

There was clapping and whistling at this.

"Welcome to the eighty-fifth Copper Mountain Rodeo!"

Louder clapping and whistling. Amy found herself joining in and so did Chet.

"We're going to start by thanking a load of volunteers and local businesses. It's their hard work and financial contributions that make our rodeo weekend such a success. And I want to begin by presenting the Marietta citizen award."

The crowd hushed, waiting to hear who would win the honor.

"This year it goes to someone I'm confident to say we all know. Someone who is always vigilant about the safety of our citizens, the first to welcome newcomers, and the person to call when you want to know the latest news in our town. Citizens of Marietta, I give you…Carol Bingley!"

Amy didn't know whether to laugh or groan. Carol Bingley seemed equally surprised. She dropped the fork she'd been using to serve fruit and then scrambled to pick it up from the ground.

"Leave the fork, Carol, and come get your award," Chelsea urged.

It seemed to Amy that the applause was uneven as Carol took the stage. She glanced around at the people near her. Some looked astonished or amused, while others exhibited rueful admiration.

She turned to smile at Chet, but discovered he was gone. She stood up for a better look, to no avail. He'd disappeared. She understood this was an important day and he needed to take care of his horses. But she wished he'd said goodbye and given her a chance to wish him luck that afternoon.

Up on stage Carol finished her acceptance speech, which had been blessedly short—probably because she'd had no time to prepare. People began to clap and, noticing Amy standing, those around her rose out of their seats too. Soon Carol was receiving a standing ovation.

Chapter Sixteen

ONCE CHET WAS gone the pancake breakfast didn't feel like fun anymore so Amy headed back to Bramble House. Even the atmosphere, which Amy had initially found warm and friendly, cooled considerably without him. Amy knew the changes had more to do with her feelings for Chet—and how she felt about herself when she was with him.

Somehow around Chet she recaptured the old Amy—the person she had been before the accident, before losing her mom and injuring her leg. She had her old confidence and joie de vie. Without him she deflated into the B & B owner who couldn't do anything right.

She cringed remembering that moment in her dining room when everyone had fallen silent after D. W. praised her coffee. She hoped he remembered his promise to rate her B & B five stars, because she knew the others sure wouldn't.

The saddest part was she liked her guests so much. She'd wanted to provide all of them with the best experience possible. And it hurt that she'd let them down.

Back at the B & B she ran into David Wilcox coming

down the stairs.

"I thought you were at the pancake breakfast."

"I was, but after my interview with Graham, I realized I'd forgotten my phone." He held it up for her to see before slipping it into his pocket. "I'm going shopping now. My wife will kill me if I don't come home with some Copper Mountain Chocolates. Will I see you later at the rodeo?"

Amy suddenly felt sick to her stomach. They were alone in the B & B. She would never find a better time.

"Actually, D. W., could I talk to you?" She had to do this now.

"Sure." He checked his watch. "Will it take long? I promised to meet some old buddies for coffee before the rodeo."

"I'm not sure."

He cocked his head. "You're being mysterious."

"Please sit down." She gestured toward the furniture in the sitting room. Once D. W. settled into one of the big armchairs, she perched on the edge of a nearby sofa. Before sitting she'd pulled out the object she'd placed in her pocket that morning. Now she rubbed the silver with her thumb, wishing she had planned exactly what to say or at least where to start.

"I have something to say that may shock you. I hope it won't be a bad shock. In fact some things you've said make me believe you already suspect."

She glanced from the bracelet to D. W.'s face, hoping to

see a glimmer of understanding in his strong-boned face.

But he was frowning and his gaze was locked on the object in her hands. She doubted he had heard a word she'd said.

"Can I see that?"

He held out his hand and reluctantly she passed him the bracelet. It looked impossibly dainty in his large, callused hands. She watched as he turned it this way, then that. Finally he glanced up at her.

"This is a lot like a bracelet I gave to a girl once. The girl I was telling you about this morning."

"It's not like it. It is it." Her hands were trembling now. Not just her hands, but her entire body. But since it was most notable in her hands, she shoved them under her thighs. Then she forced herself to take a deep breath because D. W. was still staring at the bracelet.

"This is Helen's? Helen Arden's?"

The room was so quiet she could hear the sound of her own breath going in and out of her body. "Yes."

"So then you're Helen's daughter? I thought you looked familiar. When you said you were from New York the thought crossed my mind, but only for a second. It seemed too far-fetched." He paused as his mind made an important connection. "You told me your mother died in a car accident. So Helen must be dead."

"Yes."

"That's so sad. She was so smart your mother. And she

had so much vitality. What a terrible tragedy." He passed her back the bracelet. "I'm sorry for your loss, Amy. But I'm still confused. Why didn't you tell me this earlier? I mean, wow, what a coincidence that I happened along. When did you figure out I even knew your mother?"

Amy realized she'd hoped there would be a lightning-bolt moment when she began this story. That D. W. would figure out right away that she was his daughter. His confusion made her less sure of herself.

"I-I knew about you before I met you, D. W. For most of my life you were only a name. It wasn't until after my mother died that I found the jewelry box for her bracelet. It was embossed with the name of the jewelry shop here in Marietta."

D. W. got up from the chair and strode to the window. He raked his hair off his forehead, then looked like he was trying to pull it all out by the roots. "You came to Marietta because of a jewelry box?"

"I moved here for many reasons." How to untangle all the threads. Amy wished again she'd planned this better. "One of those reasons was to find you."

"You came to find me," he repeated, his voice dull.

"When I was a kid my mother told me my father's name. But nothing else. David Wilcox is a very common name. I didn't have any context until I found that jewelry box."

D. W. swallowed. "I'm your father?"

She nodded.

He swallowed again. Then his eyes narrowed. "How old are you?"

She gave him her birthdate, feeling miserable. This wasn't how the conversation was supposed to go. He was supposed to be overjoyed. Or at least happy. But he looked like she was giving him the worst news of his life.

"Why didn't Helen tell me she was pregnant?"

"She told me she wrote you a letter." Not many people owned cell phones back in 1997. Snail mail was more common. "She admitted she didn't try too hard to find you. You were both so young and you lived on opposite sides of the country. So she decided to raise me on her own."

D. W. paced to the fireplace. Then back to the window. When he started talking again Amy wasn't sure if it was to her or if he was just thinking aloud.

"After high school I spent a few years not taking life too seriously. This was before I made the decision to work at the family ranch. I was on the circuit, but between rodeos I spent a lot of time camping and hiking. It was during one of those trips that I met Helen."

Amy kept still. She didn't want to distract him or miss a single word he was saying.

"We were only together for a few weeks, and we spent most of that time in Yellowstone and the Grand Tetons, but we did travel through Marietta and stopped here for lunch. After lunch Helen wanted to check out some shops. While she was doing that, I went to the jewelry store and bought that bracelet. It was a lot of money for me back then. But I had fallen hard for Helen. I thought I could convince her to stay in Montana. More fool me."

He stopped talking and stopped moving. Though he appeared to be looking out the window, Amy could tell his gaze was more inward looking. She gave him a few moments with his memories then said softly, "My mother wore that bracelet every day. It was her favorite piece of jewelry."

He glanced at the bracelet which she was still holding. Then back out the window. "I wonder what happened to her letter? My mother must have forgotten to give it to me. I didn't spend much time at home in those days. Maybe it accidentally got thrown away."

Since his parents were dead, they would never know the answer.

"What do you think you'd have done if you'd read it?"

"Gone to see Helen, for sure. Tried to talk her into getting married. Which would have ended in disaster. She loved New York. I could never live anywhere but here." He sighed. "Helen would have figured all that out faster than me. I guess I understand why she didn't try too hard to find me…"

He paused, and then, for the first time in their long conversation he looked at Amy. Really looked at her.

Abruptly he turned away. Not to the window this time, or the fireplace. He headed for the stairway, pausing on the first step.

"I'm sorry, Amy. I'm probably handling this terribly. But

I need to go home. Need to see my wife."

"What about the afternoon rodeo?" As soon as she asked the question, Amy realized how inane it was. After the bombshell she'd dropped, what did one small-town rodeo matter?

AMY WAS IN the kitchen when D. W. left. Clearing up from morning coffee with hands that still weren't very steady. She heard him come down the stairs, the clink of his key as he dropped it on the front desk, then the front door opening and closing. He didn't try to find her to say goodbye. Didn't even call out a farewell as he left.

Amy went to the front window to watch as he drove away. She hung back in the shadows so he wouldn't see her.

Would she ever see him again?

Did she want to?

It was only when her shoulders started heaving that she realized she was crying. She went up to the third-floor suite and threw her mother's bracelet on the floor. Then she threw herself on the bed.

What an idiot she'd been to think her existence would be good news for D. W.

She'd been an even bigger idiot to move to Montana. To buy this B & B. Her life was a mess, a total mess, and to really cap it off, she'd followed her mother's footsteps and fallen in love with a cowboy she could never have.

CHET WAS IN the box, on Hunter again, because when a horse is hot, unless they're too tired, you don't mess with a good thing. He'd been tense before yesterday's go, but today he was full-on nervous. His father had spoken to him just minutes earlier, giving more of his unwanted and unneeded advice. Now Chet could sense his father's eyes on him, watching for the smallest mistake. Though his father should want Chet to win—there'd be more money for his medical bills—there was something perverse in the old man that enjoyed seeing his son fail.

Chet looked out at the stands, searching the area where he'd seen D. W. and Amy yesterday. Today he could see neither of them. Maybe they were in different seats? He scoured the crowds but with no luck.

The seconds were ticking down. The calf was ready. Everyone was waiting for him to give the nod.

Yet he felt frozen.

What if this was the time something went terribly wrong? What if he hurt the calf or his horse or even himself?

What was he even doing here? Pretending to be a world-class cowboy, trying to be more than what he was born to be…Walt Hardwick's son.

All his hopes for his future seemed futile now. He was

willing to go through the operation and give the man a kidney. But what would happen next? The old man was going to need help, probably, and who else could give it but him?

So much for his dream of buying his own place, building a new life.

So much for the even bigger dream of finding someone to share that life with. Someone like Amy.

What did it really matter how he did in the tie-down roping? Even if he won it wouldn't change anything. Yeah, he'd win the purse but he already had a good amount of money saved up. What he needed wasn't money. It was people to love, people who loved him back.

And he didn't see how he was ever going to get that.

Chapter Seventeen

AMY DIDN'T KNOW what propelled her to get up from her bed, wash her face, and hurry down to the fairgrounds before Chet's event. On her way out, she grabbed the ticket D. W. had left on her desk with the key. The sight of the key gave her heart another pang, but she was done with crying.

Rather than walking she drove her car to save time. The rodeo announcer was introducing Chet as she rushed to her seat, and when she sat down she could see Chet and his horse were already in the box.

Something was wrong though. Hunter seemed agitated and Chet wasn't focused. He took off his hat and scrubbed a hand through his hair. Amy slid to the edge of her seat and tried to figure out what had him so upset.

She scanned the faces of the cowboys around the box and the chute where the calf was loaded and ready to go. They were all looking at Chet, waiting for his signal. But Chet was looking at someone else… She followed his gaze to a skinny, older man, wearing a battered cowboy hat.

Walt Hardwick.

Had Chet's father been playing mind games with him again? Instinctively Amy jumped to her feet and yelled as loud as she could, "Yay, Chet!"

CHET WAS SERIOUSLY tempted to back out of his event. And then he thought he heard someone holler his name. Once again he looked in the area where Amy had been sitting yesterday. This time she was there, standing with both hands waving in the air, calling out his name.

He had a sudden flashback to the day he'd given her that first riding lesson. She'd been scared. Terrified. But then she'd made a leap of faith and jumped on that horse. She'd chosen to be brave rather than scared and he could still hear her laugh of joy.

That was what he had to tap into. Erase all thoughts of the future, of the burden that was his father. Do this for his horse, for himself, for the good old-fashioned fun of it.

IT DIDN'T SEEM possible Chet had heard her. The grandstands were noisy and Amy was at least fifty yards away from the box, but Chet turned in her direction. She shouted out his name again and suddenly he was sitting more erect in his saddle. He adjusted the pig rope in his mouth, urged Hunter to the front of the box.

And then he nodded.

Less than a second later the calf was running into the arena, releasing the barrier to the box where Chet and his horse were waiting.

The rest happened so fast Amy was sure Chet beat his previous time. She waited anxiously after Chet tied the calf's legs. His run would be disqualified if the calf broke free too soon.

But Chet's knot held after he'd remounted.

"And that was as picture-perfect as they come, folks," the announcer said. "Six point eight. It's more than enough to guarantee first place for this cowboy from Boulder, Colorado."

As the crowd cheered and whistled, Chet acknowledged them by raising his hat. Before riding out of the arena, he shot a glance her way and smiled.

It was only at that point that Amy realized she was still standing. She turned to apologize to the people sitting behind her, not the Carrigans today but an older, gray-haired couple.

"I'm sorry, I was blocking your view."

Neither one of them looked perturbed and the woman said, "Don't be sorry. It was an exciting ride. Is he your fella?"

"Just a friend."

Friend was a lame word to describe how she felt about

Chet. How could she care so much for a man she'd known such a short time?

But she did care. And she was thrilled for him that he'd won. Ten thousand dollars was a lot of money. Even more than the money, she was glad he had the affirmation that his talent and his hard work were appreciated.

She stayed to watch the barrel racing, to cheer on Ruby. But once again the local girl, Willow McBride, came out on top.

Amy was surprised to find how much she enjoyed the rodeo. She would have stayed to the end if it wasn't for the mountain of laundry waiting for her at Bramble House. Not to mention bathrooms needing cleaning, cookies to be baked and tomorrow's breakfast to prep.

She left her seat and the bleachers, pausing briefly at the mini donut stand. Jo O'Neil and Ella Gilbert were in the line-up, Jo in a denim dress and boots and Ella in a checkered top and skirt. Both women glanced away quickly when they saw her. Amy decided to walk on.

She didn't have time for donuts, and they wouldn't taste as good if she couldn't share them with Chet anyway.

She was passing the beer tent when a man with a cigarette in one hand and a plastic tumbler in the other crossed her path suddenly and stumbled, almost spilling his beer.

"Watch where you're going, lady."

She recognized him then, though his hat should have given his identity away sooner.

"You're Chet's father." Even from a few feet away she could smell the alcohol on him. This wasn't his first drink of the afternoon—that was for sure.

"I am." The man's eyes narrowed as he gave her a once-over. "And you're that chick from that fancy Bramble House."

Her better sense told her not to engage, to keep walking. But she was too outraged. "Should a man with kidney disease be drinking beer and smoking?"

"What's any of that to you?"

"Nothing at all. Except haven't you asked Chet to be your kidney donor?"

The man's face paled. "That's between me and my son."

"True enough." There was so much more to be said to this man. But none of it would faze him. She might as well save her breath.

CHET HAD HOPED to catch Amy before she left the fairgrounds. He'd bought her a bag of the donuts she liked, thought maybe they could share them the way they'd done yesterday. But she had left early, before he went up on stage with the other winners to collect his check.

Huck Jones from Wyoming was the big, all-around winner, but Chet was happy with his ten grand. Normally he would set some aside for taxes and invest the rest, the way he advised others to do. But this time he was putting it all into his savings account so it would be ready for whatever unpleasant news awaited him from Walt's doctor.

He was pissed at himself for letting his father get into his head before his go that afternoon. And thankful Amy had been there to set him straight. He knew she was behind on her work at Bramble House and suspected she had come to the rodeo just to see him. Which was damn sweet of her. Much sweeter than he deserved.

His packed duffel bag was already in his truck. All he needed to do was hand over his room key, then come collect his horses and hit the road. The trip back to Bramble House could have been avoided if he'd left his key at the front desk this morning. But he'd wanted an excuse to see Amy one more time. To say goodbye.

And it would have to be a real goodbye.

Under different circumstances he might have tried to see her again. Invited her to come to one of his rodeos. Or worked out a date he could make it back to Marietta. But none of that would be fair to Amy.

This morning his father had sent him a message that he had a doctor's appointment scheduled in Phoenix two days from now. Chet figured he'd drive as far as Idaho Falls today, then push for Vegas the next day. He had a buddy in Nevada who'd agreed to board his horses so he could drive into Phoenix for his father's two o'clock appointment.

What happened next would depend on what the doctors

said.

Right now, it felt like it would be a life sentence for him.

Chet was making his way toward the exit, when he ran into Sage and Dawson. Sage grinned at him, then enveloped him in a big hug.

"You were incredible out there today. Congratulations on your win!"

Dawson clasped his shoulder. "Yeah, buddy. Well done."

"Hunter did great, too," Sage said. "All the work you put into your horses really pays off. You make a terrific team."

"Thanks." Some cowboys basked in praise, for Chet it always made him feel awkward.

"So where to next?" Sage asked.

"I was planning to head to Wyoming and then California. But there's a family emergency, so I'm going to Phoenix instead."

"A family emergency huh?" Dawson looked from him to Sage.

They both knew the only family he had left was his old man. But neither one of them asked for specifics and he didn't offer any.

"I hope you'll come back to Marietta for next year's rodeo," Sage said. "I promise we'll have a room for you. Then we can have a proper visit. I feel like we hardly got to see you this time."

"Bramble House was fine." Better than fine thanks to Amy. "Not sure if I'll still be rodeoing next year."

"Always good to retire injury free, with enough time to start a new career," Dawson agreed. "Especially for a smart guy like you."

No one had called him smart before. Maybe his grandma, when he was eight years old. But no one since.

"I've heard how helpful you've been giving saving and investing advice to the younger cowboys," Sage said. "Have you thought about going into financial planning full time?" Sage said. "You'd be genius at that."

"I've thought about it," he admitted. Lately it seemed a lot of signs were pointing in that direction. He had the start-up cash and the wherewithal to develop a business plan. But first he had to help his old man with his health crisis. And who knew how much of his nest egg would be left after that.

AMY HAD STRIPPED the linens and towels from D. W.'s room and was cleaning the bathroom when she heard someone enter the front door. She hurried down the stairs, thinking it might be Chet, but it was the Lancasters.

"Hey, Amy, I'm just going to our room to grab our bags," Fred said. "Thanks for letting us leave them here."

"You're welcome. I hope you have a safe trip home."

Sue held up two travel mugs. "We were going to fill these for the road. Do you have any fresh coffee made?"

"Yes. Help yourself." Thankfully she'd made a pot before

going upstairs, plus she'd put out some apples and cookies. But the cookies were from a package and Amy cringed inwardly as Sue looked at them and then passed.

"I saw Ruby compete," Amy said. "She was awesome."

"We're really proud," Sue agreed, as she doctored their coffees with cream and sugar. "But Ruby isn't happy unless she's winning. Hopefully she'll have better luck next time."

"Is she off to another rodeo, then?"

"Not until next year. We're heading back to Spokane now. Ruby will focus on her riding school for the fall and winter and we'll go back to our day jobs."

Sue was putting the lids on the travel mugs when Fred came back with their bags. He set one down in order to hand Amy the room key.

"Thanks for everything."

"Yes, thanks, Amy. I know we've been among your first guests so I took the liberty of making a few suggestions," Sue said. "I've left the list on the bureau in our room."

Amy cringed again. Not one suggestion or two, but *a list*. "Thanks, Sue. I hope you and Fred will come again if you're ever back this way."

Their polite smiles told her it wasn't likely.

Amy was putting a load of towels into the washing machine when she heard the doc crew arrive. They came in talking and laughing, obviously in a jubilant mood. She heard them tromp upstairs and she just had time to refresh the coffee when they were back again with their luggage, ready to go.

"How was filming today?" she asked.

"Spectacular," Rick said. "I got some wild footage in the rodeo ring."

"And we landed a quick interview with D. W. and Huck Jones, as well," Graham said.

"The only person on my list we missed was Chet Hardwick." Lucy snapped her fingers. "But I guess you can't get them all. Anyway, we've got more than enough material to work with."

"How long before your documentary is ready to air?"

"We're done with the filming, but we've got a lot of culling and editing to do. We're hoping to submit to the Austin Film Festival in March."

"Well good luck with that. I look forward to watching it one day." She held out her hand to accept their room keys. "Do you have travel mugs? You're welcome to take coffee for the road and some snacks if you want."

They stepped into the sitting room and glanced at the offerings on the side table. Rick took a handful of cookies, but Lucy and Graham declined.

"Uh, no, that's fine," Lucy said. "We'll grab something from the Java Café on our way out of town."

Amy had a lot of regrets watching them leave. A favorable review or mention on social media from that group would have been tremendously helpful to her business. But the best she could hope for was that they didn't post anything too negative.

As she put their room keys into their proper slots in the desk's bottom drawer, Amy realized that now all her guests had checked out except Chet.

And then she heard footsteps on the porch.

Chapter Eighteen

STEPPING OUT TO the porch in the bright sunshine Amy was reminded of her first impression of Chet. He looked now as he had looked to her then, like a Hollywood perfect cowboy. Hat set just so, squared chin, and lean, muscular body. When he saw her, he took off his hat and swept his fingers through his thick, dark hair.

"Thank you for coming to cheer me on at the rodeo. I almost choked. I've never done that before, but I swear if I hadn't heard you cheering in the stands…"

"It's your father. He talked to you right before your go, right?"

"Yeah."

"He's toxic, Chet. I know you feel obliged as his son to help him. But your debt has been paid. You need to get him out of your life."

He fingered the brim of his hat. "Nothing I'd like more, Amy. But I have to be able to live with myself." He paused, then glanced at her wrists. "You're wearing your bracelet again. Did you talk to D. W.?"

She swallowed hard. "I talked. Told him everything. He

was pretty shocked. And not in a good way."

Chet considered all that before answering. "Well, I can see a guy would be taken aback. Next time you see him he'll—"

"I don't think there'll be a next time. He quizzed me pretty hard about my mother, like he didn't believe he could be my father, or he didn't want to believe. And then he just took off. Wouldn't even stay to watch the finals."

"Maybe he just needs time to process. Still, that's not the reaction I expected from him. I'm sorry, Amy."

She could see the genuine caring in his expressive eyes, and it almost made her cry again. "Me too."

For a long moment neither of them said anything. Then Chet handed her his key and she slipped it into the back pocket of her jeans.

"So you're going." She stated this like the fact it was and he nodded.

"Hope to make Idaho Falls before dark."

"On route to Phoenix?"

He nodded again.

So he was going through with his plan to help his father. She wasn't surprised. She thought about sharing her brief exchange with Walt, but what was the point? She couldn't talk Chet out of what he was about to do. It made her both crazy and also love him all the more. Not that she was going to tell him how she felt. She didn't want to lay that burden on him.

Even though she suspected he was beginning to feel the same way about her.

"I don't like goodbyes," Chet said. "Just promise me one thing, Amy."

She held her breath.

"Keep taking those riding lessons. Explore the wilderness. You'll love Montana if you give it a chance."

It was good advice, but not what she'd hoped from him. She stepped forward and placed her hands on either side of his face. "You have to make me a promise too. Remember you are a good man. One of the very best."

Then she kissed him.

And let him go.

IT WAS TOO painful to watch Chet drive away so Amy went back into the house. She closed the door then leaned her back against it. Tears were prickling her eyes and she wanted nothing more than to run upstairs and fall sobbing into her bed again.

Two men leaving her in one day.

Surely, at the very least, she deserved another good cry and maybe a glass of wine and a long soak in the tub.

But very soon—in fact any moment now—four couples and two singles were going to be checking into Bramble House and not one of her rooms was ready yet. There was so much to do, all that laundry, all that cleaning, not to mention the baking and cooking. She didn't know where to turn first.

She shouldn't have gone to the rodeo, not yesterday and definitely not today. She probably should have skipped the pancake breakfast as well. But what kind of life was it if she never had time off? Even at her high-pressured job in finance she hadn't worked the number of hours she worked here.

The dryer buzzer sounded, jolting her back to reality.

Get moving, she told herself. *Moaning about your work won't get it done.*

And then she heard more footsteps on the front porch. Not one person this time, a group. Oh man, this was probably someone wanting to check in. What was she going to tell them?

Amy took a deep breath and opened the door slowly.

But it wasn't her guests on the front porch. It was Sage Carrigan. And beside her, still dressed up for the rodeo, were the women who had resigned on Amy's very first day at Bramble House: Ella Gilbert and Jo O'Neil. Amy felt ambushed. Had word gotten out about what a bad job she was doing? Were they here to run her out of town?

She noticed both Ella and Jo were checking out the porch, which needed sweeping. And the potted annuals were drooping again. Beyond the porch, the lawn once more needed mowing and presumably the perennials still needed dividing and the shrubs trimming.

"I'm sorry." She threw up her hands. "I know Bramble House is a mess, but I can't do it all. Actually, I'm not sure I can do any of it."

No sense pretending otherwise. The negative reviews, which were undoubtedly going to start appearing on social media soon, would make her failure all too public.

Sage looked from Ella to Jo, clearly expecting one of them to speak. Finally Ella stepped forward.

"We may have been a bit hasty throwing in the towel."

"It's just that we love Bramble House," Ella said. "We don't want it stripped of its history and charm."

"I'm sure that wasn't Amy's intention when she proposed some changes," Sage interjected. "Was it, Amy?"

"To be honest, after reading Eliza's book on the Brambles, I've changed my mind about some of the ideas I shared with Ella and Jo my first day here. I still think naming the rooms on the second floor after colors is lame. But rather than the generic names I'd originally proposed—I'd like to name them after specific Bramble family members and Marietta landmarks."

"That's not a bad idea," Ella said.

Amy was encouraged. "The wheelchair-accessible room on the main floor is already the Mable room. So I thought the large suite known as Red room could be the Henry and May Bell room. The room over garage could be the Twins' Retreat and the other three rooms could be Montana Sapphire, Copper and Snowbound."

"Those are great names," Jo conceded. "But are you still planning to get rid of all the family photos?"

In their first meeting she'd told Jo and Ella that she wanted to replace them with photographs of nearby Yellowstone and the Grand Tetons. But Penny's interest in the Bramble family had convinced her that this was history the general public cared about.

"No. I've changed my mind there too. I want to restore the originals, make copies for family members and then frame them with excerpts from Eliza's book."

"That would be lovely," Sage said.

"Any other changes?" Ella asked suspiciously.

"Not really…except all the rooms need painting. I'll use heritage colors of course."

"Those sound like great ideas to me," Sage said. "What do you say, ladies?"

Jo and Ella exchanged looks. Then they both nodded.

"We're here to help," Ella said. "That is, if you'll give us our jobs back."

These women had left her in the lurch, but they'd also worked loyally for Bramble House for many years and Amy was not the sort to hold a grudge. "That would be fantastic. But you should know what you're getting into. I've got a full house—expecting my guests at any minute—and none of the rooms are ready. The laundry is piled up, there are no cookies or fruit for snacking and I haven't given a thought to tomorrow's breakfast."

"Oh, that doesn't faze us," Ella said. "If you excuse me, I'll get right on those rooms." She stepped past Amy into the house.

"And I took the liberty of bringing some groceries," Jo said. "My husband will bring them in." She waved at a tall, large man leaning against a 4Runner parked on the other side of the road. Amy had been so focused on their conversation she hadn't noticed him.

"I'll make some iced tea and a charcuterie board," Jo continued. "That way, if the guests arrive before their rooms are ready they'll have something to eat. Oh, and one more thing."

"Yes?" This was happening so fast Amy was struggling to keep up.

"We brought Robert with us. He's getting the mower from the garage. When he's done with the lawn he'll tackle the caraganas. They're really looking untidy. I'm surprised Carol Bingley hasn't complained."

With that, Jo also disappeared inside. Amy and Sage stepped to the side as Jo's husband approached with the large bags from the local market.

"This is Jay," Sage said.

"Hey, Amy. You look stressed," Jay said, in a good-natured tone. "Don't you worry. Ella and my Jo have got this. Excuse me, I'll just take these to the kitchen."

"Wow," Amy said. She turned to Sage, who had clearly orchestrated this intervention. Amy didn't know how to thank her. "Can I hug you?"

Sage laughed and stepped in with open arms. "Of course."

After the hug Amy said, "You may have just saved my life."

"It works both ways, Amy. Jo's husband is a trucker with back issues and Ella's a single mom, so they really need these jobs. But Bramble house is about more than a salary to them. They really care about the place."

And so did she, Amy realized. When she'd moved here the B & B had been a business opportunity, a change of pace, an opportunity to find her father.

But the old house had grown on her, as had the town and the cowboy culture it was built on.

"Have you heard from Chet? Has he checked out yet?" Sage asked.

Amy dropped her gaze, not wanting Sage to see the raw emotion she still felt about Chet leaving. "Yes. He wants to get to Idaho Falls tonight. I think that's what he said."

"He told us he has a family emergency. I suppose it has something to do with that poor excuse of a father of his. You know our dad, Hawksley, wasn't the warmest, but compared to Walt he wins father of the year."

"I noticed a real difference in Chet once his father arrived," Amy agreed. "That man really crushes Chet's spirit."

"Yes. It's too bad Walt had to show up in town. Dawson and I were hoping... Well, Chet doesn't let many people get close. But it seemed the two of you…"

Amy hesitated. She didn't know Sage that well. But she did know Sage and Dawson were good friends of Chet's and that their concern for him was genuine. "At first we were," she admitted. "At least I think we were. But like I said, Chet changed when Walt showed up."

"It's such a shame."

"Yes." Amy could hear the vacuum cleaner start up inside. She put a hand on the door. "I should go inside and help."

"If I were you, I'd leave them to it. They're a well-oiled machine when it comes to Bramble House. And I bet you could use a break from all that cleaning and cooking."

After Sage left, Amy allowed herself a moment to relax in her favorite wicker chair. She felt tremendously relieved, but also terribly sad, and not really sure what to do with herself. She decided she could at least water the flowers and as she went along the side of the house to get the hose, she saw Robert at work on the lawn.

The short, wiry man waved but the motor was too loud for them to talk. Amy supposed she'd chat with him later about his hourly rate. Right now she was just grateful that, finally, Carol Bingley would have no reason to complain about the state of affairs at Bramble House.

Amy was sweeping the porch when the first of her expected guests arrived in a large SUV. Two couples in their late fifties got out. Amy soon found out they were good friends who often traveled together.

"I'm sorry, we're running a bit behind because of the rodeo," Amy said. "Would you mind waiting in the sitting room for a bit? I can get you some refreshments."

The four conferred and decided that was fine. Amy led them inside and was pleasantly surprised to see a pitcher of iced tea and a beautiful charcuterie board already set out on the side table.

"This looks fabulous," one of the ladies said.

"We have wine with us," her husband added. "Do you have a corkscrew?"

"Certainly." Amy put out wineglasses with the corkscrew. "Can I get you anything else?"

"This is perfect," the second lady said. Her husband was looking at the books on the coffee table. "Look, a history of this house."

"He's a history buff," his wife confided to Amy.

"We've got some other books in the library he might be interested in," Amy said. "That's the room on the other side of the foyer. Feel free to browse as much as you'd like." It was so nice to have time to chat and visit with her guests without feeling she had a dozen other tasks that needed her attention.

Jo came down the stairs then and gestured to her. "I've got the Blue and Brown rooms ready—or should I say Montana Sapphire and Copper?" She gave a cheeky grin.

"Already? You're amazing, Jo, thanks." Amy pulled the

appropriate keys out of the drawer and went to hand them to her guests.

By seven o'clock all her guests had shown up and were settled in their rooms. Jo and Ella had gone home for the day, with Ella having prepped breakfast for the following day and promising to be back at seven the next morning.

What a difference having a staff made, Amy thought as she caught up on paperwork. At eight she took a cup of tea out to the porch to enjoy the sunset.

But she couldn't relax.

Even the view didn't inspire her tonight.

It was like the colors had gone out of the sky and the mountains and the river without Chet here to enjoy them with her.

Remembering she still had his room key in her back pocket, Amy decided to check out his old room. Maybe now that she had a staff, she'd have time to finish painting it. Then she opened the door and found the job had already been done.

She turned on the light and admired the fresh new look. The room looked so much larger and cleaner. The green tape was gone. He'd even touched up the baseboards.

When had Chet possibly found the time to do all this?

He'd left the paint cans and supplies in a neat pile in the far corner of the room. As she looked over the rest of the room, she realized he'd washed his bedding—where she had no idea, he must have gone to a laundromat—and remade the bed. He'd also left his washroom spick and span.

Tears came then, first filling her eyes then spilling down to her cheeks. This was his goodbye gift to her. He was not ever coming back.

How was it that the best day she'd had at Bramble House had suddenly also become the worst?

Chapter Nineteen

CHET DIDN'T GET to Idaho Falls until almost nine. It had been a difficult drive. Usually he enjoyed being on the road but he couldn't shake the suspicion that he was headed in the wrong direction. Away from Amy instead of toward.

He'd had to take care of his horses and eat his own supper—a ham and cheese sandwich he'd bought at a gas station—in the dark. He was just pitching his tent for the night when Walt showed up in his old beater.

"Got room in that tent for me?"

No way was Chet sharing a two-man tent with his father. "You take it." He'd sleep in his truck. Wouldn't be the first time.

Chet fell asleep heartsore and bone-weary, not waking until the pre-dawn morning chorus of the local songbirds. He got out of the cab to stretch and noticed the tent's front zipper was open. Just to be sure he peeked inside. The tent reeked, but there was no sign of his old man, other than a couple of empty beer cans next to his sleeping bag. Hell, hadn't the old man heard of bears?

Chet grabbed the cans. He'd drop them into the recycling bin on his way to the toilet. But first he checked on his horses. Hunter and Bourbon were quietly munching on tufts of grass, seeming perfectly content. He patted each on the neck. "Don't worry, I'll be back soon to feed you."

He wondered how Amy was doing back at Bramble House. Had she seen the paint job he'd done in the room over the garage? He hoped it met her standards. Most of all he wondered if she'd thought of him last night when the sun was going down.

Was she missing him as much as he missed her?

Impossible.

The toilets were located in a building about a hundred yards from his campsite. As he headed for the men's side, he caught a whiff of smoke and recognized his father's brand. When he opened the door he could hear his father's voice coming from behind one of the cubicles.

"Yeah, yeah I hear you, but it's going good."

Chet froze, not wanting to betray his presence by walking inside. Why, he couldn't say. But the hairs were standing up on the back of his neck. He sensed something bad was afoot. For no reason other than he knew his father.

"I'm telling you he bought the story."

Chet stopped breathing as his hackles rose further. He had no idea who Walt was talking to but he was pretty sure that the person who had 'bought the story' was him.

After a brief pause, Walt continued, "I'll get him to come

to Arizona, make some excuses why he can't see my doctor, and then hit him up big-time. Then we'll finally have the dough we need to buy that house you want."

The revelation hit Chet like a bucket of icy water to the face. And then he wondered why he was even surprised. There was no limit to how low Walt would sink. Pretending to be sick to play on Chet's sense of obligation wasn't even the worst thing he'd ever done.

But it was going to be the last thing, Chet decided.

He stepped inside, letting the door shut behind him.

"Got to go," he heard his father whisper.

Chet relieved himself at the urinal and took his time washing his hands and face at the sink. Finally Walt opened the cubicle door.

"Oh it's you," he said. "I was just having a smoke someplace warm." He tossed his cigarette butt into the toilet and flushed.

"So who were you talking to?" Chet asked casually.

"Ah, just a friend of mine." His father kept his head averted as he headed for the door.

Chet followed right behind him. "You actually have a friend do you?"

"Very funny, smart-ass. I have more friends than you do. What time you want to hit the road? I could use some coffee. Don't suppose you brought a camp stove with you?"

"I'll be leaving right after I feed my horses. And this time I don't want you following."

"Why the hell not? No good you getting to Phoenix before me."

"I'm not going to Phoenix." It felt so good to say those words. Chet lengthened his stride, but somehow his father kept up.

"What the hell? I thought you agreed to help me?"

"Help you buy a house with that 'friend' you were talking with on the phone? Not bloody likely, old man."

An ugly red stain crept up Walt's neck. "What are you talking about a house? Are you crazy?"

"Good try. But I heard every word. You're not sick. All you want is money. My money. Big surprise." Chet was back at his truck. Ignoring Walt, he took out the buckets and feed for his horses.

"You got it all wrong."

Chet gave a brittle laugh. "I don't think so. What I got wrong was letting you leech off me all these years. If you'd been a halfway decent dad, I suppose I might have owed you. But you never provided a proper home. You cuffed me and insulted me as you dragged me along on your vagabond life. If I hadn't worked since I was ten, I wouldn't even have had enough to eat."

"At least I never abandoned you."

"Really? Sleeping alone in your truck while you were on a bender felt a lot like being abandoned. But whatever. The past is the past. What matters now is the future and the fact that you won't have any part in mine."

"What exactly are you saying?"

"I'm saying leave me alone, old man. I'm tired of dealing with your garbage. And I sure as hell am never giving you another cent, red or otherwise."

"That's not right. I know you. You're not that heartless."

"Every man has a limit, and you've found mine. Goodbye, Walt."

As Chet took care of his horses, Walt stormed around the campsite, swearing and smoking another cigarette. Finally he got into his truck and just sat there, obviously waiting for Chet to leave so he could follow.

Chet took his time with his horses. Once they were loaded, he took down the tent, intending to throw it away at the first opportunity.

Before climbing into his cab he took a deep breath of the clean morning air. He was not going to Phoenix. He was not giving up a kidney. He was not going to have to nurse his father or ever give him money again.

He smiled. What a beautiful morning. He didn't feel angry. He simply felt free.

At the ramp onto US-20 Chet signaled a right-hand turn, headed north. Behind him his father honked, then rolled down his window and cursed. But Chet ignored him.

He wasn't going to Phoenix. He was going to Wyoming.

THE NEXT MORNING Amy had the pleasant experience of serving coffee and chatting with her guests while Jo worked behind the scenes cooking breakfast. Amy would have enjoyed the experience even more if she'd been able to sleep last night.

But she'd had too much on her mind. Her father, of course. But mostly Chet. His goodbye yesterday had sounded pretty final, but she'd hoped he would send her a text message. At least let her know he'd made it to Idaho Falls okay.

But there'd been nothing.

After breakfast Amy helped Jo clean up the kitchen.

"I'm going to bake cookies for tea and then be off before noon," Jo said. "I work at the Graff Hotel most afternoons. My arrangement with Eliza was seven to eleven at Bramble House, five days a week. I'll prep breakfasts for the weekend on Friday and make sure there are lots of cookies and muffins in the freezer. Does that work for you?"

"It sounds perfect." She was definitely going to have time for riding lessons now, Amy realized. And she'd be able to spend time on marketing and promotion as well. Though it did seem Bramble House had a good reputation in the area as it was almost fully booked through October.

She could work on special offers to pull in business in the slow times, which, according to the binder, was November through April, with small bumps around Christmas, Valentine's Day and Easter.

Amy took a cup of coffee out to the porch, intending to read another chapter of Eliza's book on the Bramble family, but the yard looked so beautiful she had to pause for a few minutes to admire it.

She couldn't believe it had taken less than twenty-four hours for the Bramble House staff to take this property in hand. If only she'd been more diplomatic from the beginning, she'd have saved herself so much grief.

Carol Bingley walked by, probably on her way to the pharmacy, and gave her a wave. "Your yard looks lovely," she said.

"Thanks." A compliment from Carol Bingley. She'd better savor it.

A passing truck slowed and then came to a stop on the other side of the street. It took a moment for Amy to recognize David Wilcox's vehicle. Oh my Lord, what was he doing here?

She watched as he got out from behind the wheel, then went to open the passenger door. A woman was with him, tiny, about five feet tall, and very thin. She wore her blonde, gray-streaked hair in a bob, and had delicate, pretty features.

D. W.'s wife, Amy surmised. She stood and waited as D. W. led the woman along the walkway to her house.

"This is a surprise."

"I bet it is," D. W. said. "I'm sorry for the way I ran out yesterday, Amy. Partly I was in shock, but I also needed to talk to my wife. This is Mary Beth."

"Hi, Amy." Mary Beth met her on the porch, taking one of Amy's hands between both of hers. She had deep-set, round blue eyes, and she gazed at Amy with warmth, as if she'd already decided she liked her.

Amy felt more wary. "Nice to meet you. Would you like to sit down?"

"Thank you." The couple sat, side by side, on the double rocker.

Physically they were a mismatched pair, the petite artist, the burly rancher. But their hands were linked, and Amy could tell they were very close and very happy. D. W. had made a good match for himself, something her mother had never managed to do.

"I'm just picky," Helen had told her daughter whenever Amy asked why she never dated anyone for very long. Now Amy wondered if Helen had been looking for someone to live up to D. W. Amy would never know the answer for sure, but she supposed the way her mom had prized her silver bracelet might hold the answer.

She put a protective hand on the bracelet now, not sure why the Wilcoxes were here.

Mary Beth broke the silence. "D. W. and I have always had a policy of no secrets, Amy. It was important to the health of our relationship because we've had to spend a lot of time apart, especially when he was on the rodeo circuit."

"I get that," she said warily.

"Your news yesterday was a real bombshell, and you may

have been hurt that D. W.'s first instinct was to tell me. But that's the way we operate. We always turn to each other. He thought I might be upset, silly man. But of course his affair with your mother happened long before we were married, and after raising three sons, I'd be delighted to welcome a daughter into our family. If you'd give us that opportunity."

Amy turned to D. W., surprised to see tears in his eyes.

"Amy, I felt a fatherly connection to you from the start. But I never dreamed it was real, that you truly were my daughter. It feels like the most unexpected and undeserved blessing." He reached for her hand and squeezed it. "I'm sorry if I hurt you yesterday. It wasn't my intention."

"I-I don't know what to say."

"D. W. told me you lost your mother recently," Mary Beth said gently. "I'm real sorry honey. Forty-five is way too young to go and I know you'll always miss her. But we don't want you to feel like you're alone in this world."

"We'd love you to come out to the ranch," D. W. said. "Meet your brothers. They were pretty surprised to hear the news, but they are excited to meet you. And I'd love to spend as much time with you as I can. I've got a lot to make up for."

The tears were coming—there was no way to stop them. D. W. got up from the rocker and held out his arms. Stepping into her father's hug, Amy felt the sweetest ache. Her father. She'd finally found him. If only her mom could see them now.

Chapter Twenty

CHET DID WELL at the rodeos in Wyoming and California, but he couldn't shake the feeling that it was time to move on in his life. Maybe a financial planning business would be the best thing. He'd given a lot of advice free of charge over the years, but he'd also been told that his services were something people would be willing to pay for.

What he needed was a business plan. But every time he sat down to draft one, something inside of him resisted.

He didn't know why. He'd taken the courses; he had the degree. Being financially responsible was something he was passionate about and he enjoyed sharing his knowledge with others.

Why not make it a business?

Chet leaned back in his camping chair, set in the shade of a canyon live oak. He'd pitched his tent in the Dripping Springs Campground, near the Agua Tibia Wilderness. His horses had been fed and watered and now, with nothing to do until he went to bed, he tried to visualize himself in a new life, where he worked behind a desk as a financial planner.

He just couldn't see it.

When he thought about tomorrow, the next month, hell, even a year from now, all that came to mind was Amy and Bramble House and the prettiest town he'd ever seen.

Could he make a new life for himself in Marietta? Did he even dare to dream that Amy could be part of that life?

He patted the phone in the front pocket of his shirt. Many times, every day, he was tempted to reach out to her. Find out how she was doing. Whether she still thought of him. What stopped him was the knowledge he had nothing to offer her.

What if he started the financial planning business and it failed? Or he hated it? Then he'd be nothing but a has-been rodeo cowboy. And Amy deserved so much more than that.

So he didn't text her.

He just went to bed lonely.

WITH THE REHIRING of Jo, Ella and Robert, managing Bramble House B & B went from a head-spinning and physically exhausting challenge to the job of Amy's dreams. She now had time to catch up the books, to prepare good content for Bramble's social media accounts, and to take care of extra details, like ordering new name signs for the rooms, and getting high-quality reproductions made of the family photographs. One task she had no luck with, however, was organizing a painting crew. She supposed she would have to paint Bramble House on her own. Room by room, it would eventually get done.

One morning, just a few days after Jo had started working for her, Jo told her, "If you ever want to take a few days to yourself, my husband and I can stay here and look after the B & B for you. We used to do that for Eliza and Marshall."

"That would be wonderful. D. W. and Mary Beth have been wanting me to visit their ranch, but it's a long drive for just one day."

"Just let me know the dates you want to go," Jo said. After a brief pause, she continued, "If you don't mind my asking, is it true D. W. is your father?"

"It is." Amy told Jo the story of her mother and D. W.'s love affair. Jo listened with a soft smile on her careworn face.

"And is that the bracelet he gave her?" She pointed to the one Amy always wore.

"It sure is."

"Ah, how romantic. But also sad. You growing up without a dad and your mom never finding the right man."

"I know. But Mom had a full life. She had a successful academic career, lots of friends, and we were really close."

"That does sound like a good life. I would have loved a daughter, but me and Jay, we couldn't have children."

"I'm sorry."

"Ah, such is life. We all have our trials."

Jo's offer proved providential when the very next day D.

W. called to invite Amy to Whispering Pines for the weekend. Amy made sure to include her new cowboy boots when she packed for the overnight stay. D. W. had promised her another riding lesson.

I'm following through on my promise to you, Chet. She hoped he was remembering what he'd promised her as well, and didn't let his father's negativity weigh him down.

Her weekend at Whispering Pines was a total success. Her younger brothers were outgoing, hilarious and kind. Mary Beth was a fabulous cook with a warm, inclusive nature. And D. W. lived up to his word and took her out riding not once but twice.

During her visit D. W. also drove Amy by the Big Sky Rodeo Academy. "I'll give you an inside tour on your next visit. Mary Beth and I are damned proud of this place. Our boys all volunteer here, as well as us."

"Chet told me a little about it. You teach horsemanship and basic rodeo skills to high school aged students?"

"Yeah, but what sets our academy apart from other rodeo schools, is that we guarantee spots to kids whose parents can't afford the program. These are vulnerable young people, who need healthy direction and guidance in their lives."

"That sounds awesome," Amy said. "If it wasn't such a long drive from Marietta, I'd love to help too. Obviously not with the horses or the rodeo skills. But maybe something in the office."

D. W. shot her a sideways look. "Funny you should say

that. I've been thinking of opening another academy. That was one of the reasons I accepted the invite to the Copper Mountain Rodeo this year. Mary Beth and I think Marietta would be the perfect location for our next school."

"How exciting. You can count on me to help."

"I was hoping you would say that. But let me run another idea by you first. And you be sure to shut me down if you think I'm out of line."

Amy listened to what he had to say and had no trouble giving him her answer. Ten minutes later they were back at Whispering Pines where Mary Beth had an awesome taco lunch laid out for them.

Amy left with the promise that she would come back soon.

"You're welcome every weekend if you want," Mary Beth said. "And definitely Thanksgiving and Christmas."

"Don't think all the weekends will be like this one," Luke, the youngest said. "They'll be putting you to work before you know it."

Amy's heart felt lighter as she drove back to Marietta that Sunday afternoon. Many good things had happened the past few weeks. Though they'd had a rough start, she truly appreciated the staff at Bramble House. And she was grateful to her father and his family for their easy acceptance and affection. She looked forward to getting to know them better. She still missed her mother every day, but it was nice not to feel she was all on her own in the world.

And yet. Despite all these wonderful developments, she could not forget Chet. A dozen times a day she fought the urge to send him a text or give him a call. Since he'd been the one to leave, she thought he should be the one to reach out first.

But as the days went by, there was nothing.

Perhaps she'd misinterpreted his interest in her. Maybe he hadn't cared as much as she'd thought.

Or possibly he was just too busy taking care of his father. She was desperate to know if he was going through with his intention to donate a kidney. If so when was the surgery?

She had so many things to tell him. So many questions to ask. But mostly there was just a deep ache of loneliness, especially in the evening as the sun was going down and she was sitting on her porch watching it alone.

Chapter Twenty-One

CHET WAS STILL asleep when his phone rang. In the dark he groped the floor of the tent for his phone. Dang it was chilly out. Finally he brought his phone up to his face. Unknown caller. He hesitated, then decided to answer.

"Yeah?"

"David Wilcox here, Chet. Hope seven thirty isn't too early to call."

It was six thirty in California, not that it mattered. Chet would always have time to take a call from D. W.

"Not too early at all. What's up?" Chet put the phone on speaker, then scrambled out of his sleeping bag and reached for his jeans and shirt.

"Well, it's a bit of a long story. See Mary Beth and me had a visitor on the weekend. I believe you know her. Amy Arden from Bramble House?"

Chet froze for a moment. It was too damn early to have this many surprises sprung on him. "I know Amy, yes."

"And you also know that by some amazing miracle, she's my daughter?"

"Yup."

"The two of us got off to a shaky start. But we're good as gold now. I wanted you to know that, even though it may not have anything to do with the offer I have for you."

Chet really wished he'd had time for a cup of coffee before this phone call. Fully dressed now, he unzipped his tent and went outside, hoping the brisk desert air would help his brain function faster.

"I'm glad you and Amy worked things out. But what offer are you talking about?"

"You know about the Big Sky Rodeo Academy?"

"Yes, sir, I do." He could see the faint glow of dawn on the eastern horizon. With his phone now clamped to his ear he went to check on his horses.

"I'm thinking I'd like to open a second academy. Marietta seems like the right place. All I need is a manager. Someone who knows the rodeo world, but also someone who knows what it's like to be a kid who maybe doesn't have the best home life in the world. Sound like anyone you know?"

Chet grinned.

In that moment all the mixed-up pieces of his life came together and he could finally see a path forward. He'd take the hard lessons he'd learned as Walt Hardwick's son, and he'd use them to help other kids. He'd still be working with horses; he'd still be part of the rodeo world.

Best of all, he'd be in Marietta.

Close to Amy.

THREE WEEKS AFTER the rodeo, Amy was in the Copper Mountain Chocolate Shop picking up a new order—she'd decided to continue supporting local rather than buying bulk chocolate from Costco—when Sage had asked her if she'd like to go for a trail ride with her on the weekend.

"Oh, I'd love that. But I'm a total novice. I've only been on a horse three times."

"Chet said you were a natural. And I can give you pointers. I promise we'll start gentle."

"In that case, I'd love it."

"Great. How about we leave after lunch on Saturday and drive down to the Circle C?"

Amy was a little nervous, but things went better than she'd dared hope. She rode Moonstruck again, and Sage was a great instructor. Amy felt comfortable leaving the training corral and riding through the woods to a viewpoint on a ridge about four miles from the barns.

The foliage on the aspen and cottonwoods were at the peak of their golden autumn colors, early snow dusted the mountain tops, and the sky was a clear blue topaz. It was the most perfect day and Amy couldn't help wishing Chet were here to share it with her.

He'd been right—there was a beautiful freedom in exploring nature on the back of a horse. Riding was a better workout than she'd expected, and it left her feeling exhilarated—even greater than any runner's high she'd ever experienced.

She looked around for Sage, wanting to thank her for giving her this experience. But the red-headed rider had disappeared. Before Amy could panic, she noticed someone approaching from the distance. It was a man riding a beautiful sorrel. The sorrel had a white mark on his forehead, and the man…well he was just an outline from here, but Amy knew that silhouette.

Suddenly every muscle tensed; every nerve went on alert. She swung Moonstruck around to face the sorrel. As she urged her horse to go faster, Amy could feel her hair flying behind her.

And then she was close enough to see Chet's face. He was as handsome as she remembered, no, more so, and he was smiling. She couldn't remember ever seeing him look this happy. Not even in the rodeo ring when he'd won first place.

"What are you doing here?" She felt breathless and a little light-headed. "And what happened to Sage?"

"You've been victim of a setup," Chet admitted, his smile becoming a playful grin. "I asked Sage to bring you out here." He paused, then added, "I hope that's okay?"

She heard a note of uncertainty in that last question, and his vulnerability touched her. "I'm thrilled to see you." And she was. If they weren't on horseback she'd be throwing her arms around him right now.

Maybe that was why he'd chosen to meet her like this, she realized, to give them both some space. "But I don't understand. I thought you were in Phoenix. Where's your father?"

"I've got a lot to tell you. Are you okay to ride a bit farther along this ridge? For a city gal you sure look great on the back of a horse."

"I feel great, too. You were right, Chet. This is fantastic." She swept her arm expansively to indicate the view. But it wasn't being on horseback, the fresh air, or the beautiful autumn scenery that was lighting her up right now. She kept turning to look at Chet, hardly daring to believe he was really here. And he kept looking at her, unable to stop smiling, and she knew he was feeling the same inner glow.

They rode for a few peaceful moments, side by side, without Chet saying anything. Amy did her best to be patient. Chet would talk when he was ready.

Finally he said, "I hear you've been out to D. W.'s ranch?"

How had he heard that? She supposed Sage must have told him. "Yes, and it was wonderful. The day after you left..." she paused as her voice hitched "...D. W. came back to Bramble House with his wife. Mary Beth is amazing, Chet. She's strong, but also so warm and caring. It turned out they both wanted to welcome me to their family. And they really have."

"Sounds like you really connected."

"Yes. You'd think it would be awkward, having a twenty-six-year-old suddenly show up claiming to be family. But it hasn't been. Even their sons have taken it all in stride. And they're great kids. It's so amazing to find myself part of that family. It's like discovering an entirely new side of myself, as well."

"I'm happy for you. And not surprised. D. W. is one of the best. A genuinely good man."

She heard a note of bitterness creep into his voice and could guess why. "Unlike Walt."

"Unlike Walt," Chet agreed. He cleared his throat. "The day I left Marietta, I made it to Idaho Falls like I planned. I hadn't expected to travel with Walt, but he joined me there and the next morning I overheard a phone conversation."

A feeling of dread rose in her gut.

"That's when I found out his story about being sick was all a lie. He wanted to lure me to Phoenix, make excuses why I couldn't meet his doctor, and then hit me up for a big payoff. I guess he figured I'd be so relieved I didn't have to donate my kidney, I wouldn't mind parting with a good chunk of my savings."

Amy stared at him. "That is—beyond despicable. But in a weird way it's also wonderful. I'm so relieved you don't have to give him one of your kidneys."

Chet nodded. "You and me both. But it's even better than that. For the first time in my life, I feel free of that man. I've cut ties completely. There will be no more guilt. No more feeling like I owe him something."

Once more Amy had the urge to throw her arms around him. And once more she understood why Chet had needed to have this conversation on horseback. On the back of his horse, he was in his comfort zone, the one place in his crazy mixed-up life with his father, where he'd felt in control.

"Good. I'm glad to hear it." But there was so much more for him to explain. "That was almost three weeks ago. What have you been doing since then?"

"I had a competition in Wyoming, another in California. I did well in both, but my heart wasn't in it." He turned to her, holding her gaze. "I missed you too much."

Her heart leapt at that. "I've missed you too."

"You don't know how happy I am to hear that. Since the day I left Marietta, I've wanted nothing more than to come back to you, but I couldn't. Not as a washed-up cowboy with no prospects."

"I thought you were going to start a financial planning business?"

"I was toying with the idea. But it never sat right. And then I got a call from your father."

Amy tensed, hoping against hope. When D. W. had told her his plan, she'd been afraid to put too much stock in it. "And…?"

"He plans to open another Big Sky Rodeo Academy. In Marietta. And he wants me to run it."

"Chet." She could feel the hugest smile break out on her

face. "But that's wonderful! And of course you'd be perfect."

"I don't think I would have been happy with an office job. This way I get to keep working with horses and passing on the skills I've learned on the rodeo. More importantly, if I can help kids who've had a rough start in life, it means some good will come out of the years I spent at the mercy of my old man."

Amy couldn't have agreed more. But she couldn't resist adding, "It also means you'll be staying in Marietta."

"It does. I hope you're good with that?"

"Definitely."

They were back in the trees now. Chet held up his hand. "Time to turn around. But let's stop for a moment." He dismounted smoothly then went to help her. After tying the horses' reins around the white trunk of a birch tree, he reached for her hands.

"Amy."

She stared into the warmth of his chocolatey-brown eyes and felt a connection deeper than any she'd known. This man. She didn't know why he stirred her so deeply. But he had, from the first moment they'd met.

"I'm falling in love with you, Amy."

She could feel moisture gathering in her eyes. "Promise you won't leave me again?"

"Promise."

And then he kissed her. For a very long time.

Chapter Twenty-Two

Eleven Months Later: A Wedding at Bramble House

AMY STOOD IN front of the full-length mirror in her suite on the third floor of Bramble House. Mary Beth was helping her with the tiny buttons at the back of her sleeveless white eyelet dress. The bodice fitted snugly, then opened to a scalloped skirt with a romantic frill on the bottom. It paired beautifully with the turquoise boots Amy had coveted since her first—but definitely not last—visit to the Marietta Western Wear shop on Main Street.

"You look beautiful, my dear." Mary Beth squeezed her arm. "I know you must wish your mother was here. She'd be so proud, believe me."

Amy had never missed her mother more than while planning this wedding, but she'd cried those tears and she was too happy today to shed more. "I do miss my mom but thank you for being here. And for being you."

She hugged her stepmother.

"What a happy day for D. W. and me when you came into our lives," Mary Beth said. "And now for the something borrowed…" She hung a string of pearls around Amy's neck.

"D. W. bought these for me on our wedding day."

"My father does have good taste in jewelry," Amy said as she put on her silver bracelet. She hated to think what her life would have been like if her mother hadn't cherished this bracelet—and kept the box it came in. "There. I think I'm ready."

"I know you are. You look beautiful."

"Where's Chet?"

"Waiting impatiently in the back garden. Shall I tell him we're ready?"

Amy nodded.

She felt like she'd been ready since the day Chet had surprised her on that trail ride at the Circle C last September. But Chet had refused to rush her. "Let's enjoy this courtship phase."

He'd moved back into the room over the garage, insisting on paying her rent while at the same time making himself useful in numerous ways. He'd painted every square inch of the main house and had even bought a woodburning kit so he could make new signs for all the bedrooms.

He'd also helped Robert in the yard. Turned out his grandmother had taught him a few things about gardening, too, and he knew about dividing perennials and deadheading flowers. He also built a circular brick patio in the back with a firepit in the center. He'd even made the cedar chairs to go with it.

And all this while helping with the construction phase of

the new rodeo academy. They had opened their doors this summer and had been flooded with excited young applicants. True to D. W.'s word, half of the spaces were reserved for underprivileged kids, and those were the kids Chet took the most satisfaction in working with.

Life was busy, but oh so satisfying, and best of all were the evenings with Chet. They always made time to watch the sunset together. When the weather was too cold to sit on the porch, Chet built a fire in the back, and they cuddled under fuzzy blankets.

But it was late August now, and the weather was perfect, neither too hot nor too cold. After proposing in March, on the spring equinox, Chet had built a trellis in the backyard, saying, "It'll make a pretty background for wedding pictures."

Oh how she loved that man. It seemed there was nothing he couldn't do. But best of all, he was steadfast and true and for all of Montana's beauty there was no better view than gazing into his eyes.

There was a knock on the door.

"Come in," Amy said.

D. W. peeked in. Let out a low whistle. "Man, do you look like your mother right now. Ready for your old man to walk you down the aisle?"

"I am." Never in her wildest dreams had Amy imagined having her father by her side on her wedding day. Life was unpredictable, to say the least. Terrible losses could be followed by wonderful gains.

She and Chet had planned a small wedding, by choice. They'd invited Amy's half brothers, of course, as well as Jo and Ella who felt more like friends now than employees. They'd asked Sage and Dawson to act as witnesses, since if not for them they would never have met. Amy was particularly grateful to Sage for booking Chet into Bramble House. As he liked to say now, "Thank goodness you had that no-cancellation policy."

As her father led her into the garden, Amy hardly noticed the guests sitting in the lines of rented chairs. Her eyes were on Chet, her iconic cowboy, only without his hat today. He was wearing a black suit jacket, white shirt, and dark blue jeans and he looked so incredibly handsome, her knees felt weak.

D. W. kissed her cheek then released her. Chet stepped forward and took both her hands.

"Amy, you look like a goddess."

Time played tricks on Amy as they exchanged their vows. Some moments felt like they were passing in slow motion, yet the ceremony was over before she knew it.

She gazed into Chet's eyes with wonder. "I guess we're married now, Cowboy."

"I think it's going good, so far."

And then Chet kissed her. And their family and friends cheered.

Epilogue

Bramble House: 3 Stars

Charming house and comfortable beds but the owner seems a little clueless.

—Lucy_Producer

Bramble House: 5 Stars

Good Wi-Fi, free cookies and the owner is hot

—Rick_FilmMaker

Bramble House: 5 Stars

You can't do better than to stay at Bramble House. One of the best holidays of my life

—D. W._WhisperingPines

Bramble House: 4 Stars

Bramble House and the town of Marietta are both fabulous. The new B & B owner has a lot to learn, but I would stay here again.

—Sue_Hikes124

Bramble House: 5 Stars

Gorgeous historical home. We stayed here last year and to be honest, the service was uneven. But we decided to come back and are we ever glad we did. The owner had hired a wonderful cook and an impeccable cleaning woman. Best of all she has a cowboy handyman who keeps up with all the little repair jobs that come with owning a heritage home. And he's not bad to look at either. Highly recommend

—PennyWanders

The End

Thank You

I am thankful for a week in May of 2013, spent at our cottage in Flathead Lake, Montana, in the company of my most excellent friend Jane Porter, and my soon-to-become excellent friends Megan Crane and Lillian Darcy. The four of us enjoyed time on the dock and lots of cherry crisp before road tripping through Western Mountain to Livingston and Paradise Valley where we found plenty of inspiration. During this week the first four books of Tule Publishing were conceived, along with the fictional town of Marietta and the Copper Mountain Rodeo.

Now, ten years later, I'm honored to have written a ten-year anniversary book for the Copper Mountain Rodeo. Thanks to Jane, Megan and Sinclair who joined me in the small mountain town of Canmore, Alberta, to plan this series. Thanks to the Tule Publishing team of Meghan, Cyndi, Nikki, Marlene and Helena who worked their magic to turn our words into actual books. And thanks to the readers, especially the Main Street Marietta followers, who believe in our town, who love our characters, and who make everything we do worthwhile.

The 85th Copper Mountain Rodeo Series

Book 1: *Take Me Please, Cowboy* by Jane Porter

Book 2: *Tempt Me Please, Cowboy* by Megan Crane

Book 3: *Marry Me Please, Cowboy* by Sinclair Jayne

Book 4: *Promise Me Please, Cowboy* by C.J. Carmichael

Available now at your favorite online retailer!

See Carol Bingley's story in….
The Untold Story of Carol Bingley by Jane Hartley

More books by C.J. Carmichael

Letters From Grace

The Shannon Sisters series
Book 1: *A Cowboy's Proposal*

Book 2: *A Convenient Christmas Proposal*

Book 3: *A Hometown Proposal*

The Carrigans of the Circle C series
Book 1: *Promise Me, Cowboy*

Book 2: *Good Together*

Book 3: *Close to Her Heart*

Book 4: *Snowbound in Montana*

Book 5: *A Cowgirl's Christmas*

Book 6: *A Bramble House Christmas*

Bitter Root Mysteries series

Book 1: *Bitter Roots*

Book 2: *Bitter Truth*

Book 3: *Bitter End*

Book 4: *Bittersweet*

Available now at your favorite online retailer!

About the Author

USA Today Bestselling author C. J. Carmichael has written over 50 novels with more than three million copies in print. She has been nominated for the *RT Bookclub's* Career Achievement in Romantic Suspense award, and is a three time nominee for the *Romance Writers of America* RITA Award.

Thank you for reading

Promise Me Please, Cowboy

If you enjoyed this book, you can find more from all our great authors at TulePublishing.com, or from your favorite online retailer.

Made in the USA
Monee, IL
23 December 2024